tinged

the electric tunnel #3

tinged

the electric tunnel #3

rachel blaufeld

about this book

"You're not tinged, babe. Not then, not now, not ever. I love you. And you don't need the ocean water to cleanse you. Whatever crap you're spewing is just that—BS. You're perfect."

Lynx fled the Vegas Underground for Miami, desperate to uncover certain secrets of her past when she goes rogue in a dangerous world.

Michael Anthony Wind shed his pretty-boy upbringing and family legacy for his first job as a bouncer at the Electric Tunnel. Now successful in his own right, he's only missing his woman.

When she's finally found, Lynx is broken, unsure if she can be put back together. Mike may be strong, but is he strong enough for the job?

Their story isn't beautiful or safe, but it's theirs. Two tortured souls colored by their past, looking to paint a different future.

about this book

This book is for the few readers who took a risk on me from day one— when I was nothing but a one-book nobody. Thank you for continuing to believe in me.

Part One

Part One

prologue

LYNX PEERED out the window, gathering the long pale pink drape in her hand and pulling it back to reveal a never-ending blue sky with run-down buildings and mosques littering the horizon. Focusing on the bright fireball, she allowed the sun to warm her for a moment. Then she squeezed her eyes tight, blocking the light, her heart a black Arabian stallion galloping in a dusty ring, her eyelids a heavy dam for the tears she wouldn't allow herself to shed.

She'd absolutely forbidden herself to cry.

Turning her hand, she opened her eyes and glanced at the small scabbed-over indentations where she'd dug her own fingernails into her palm to stop the salty flow from escaping. Tiny crescent moons—both faint and recently crusted over—created their own patterns like constellations in the sky. Lynx could get lost in the labyrinth before her, searching for some hidden meaning.

But she didn't.

The heavy curtain fluttered closed behind her as she turned and took in the grandeur of her surroundings. Tapestries woven in rich jewel tones adorned the walls, and soft wool rugs covered the floors. Lynx ran her hand along the sumptuous satin lining of the chaise she

1

lay on and forced her panic to flee with her breath.

Never in a million years had she dreamed of living in such opulence, and yet here she was in the middle of this palatial room, clothed in designer garments and draped in emeralds and sapphires.

There was no reason to cry. She was extremely special, and this was her home.

Or so she was told.

one

Miami

PULLING MY convertible out of the Wave's lot at two o'clock in the morning, I turned my metallic-white baby toward the beach as the ocean waves slapped in the distance in the dark night. I told myself to go home, but knew I wouldn't listen. Instead I did the same thing I'd done several nights a week for the last year.

I headed for a drive.

As much as I needed to clear my head, unwind, and allow Miami's humid ocean breeze to wash over me, it wasn't that type of drive.

It was a mission. One I shouldn't be on, definitely a self-appointed assignment I should drop. Immediately. I was a renegade on a journey to hell because my assignment would certainly only end in heartbreak and pain.

Oh well. *Fuck it.*

I drove along Washington Avenue, scanning the sidewalks. Block after block, I noted bar crawlers on a crazy Saturday night, party-goers on a mission, and vacationers out for a good time. But tourists weren't who I was here to see.

Narrowing my focus to the locals, I searched for a familiar face. When I saw who I was looking for, I pulled over, shifted into park, and climbed out of the small sports car. After patting my little lady's door for good measure, I took casual strides down the street, pretending to be out looking for a good time.

"Hey, Chantilly, how you doing, girl?" I wrapped my arm around the shoulders of a tall, curvy blonde clad in black leather and lace, walking confidently on mega-heels.

"Heya, Mikey baby. How ya doing, tough guy?" she said, pulling me in for a hug.

There I was, Michael Wind, *Big Mike*, the prep-school-educated bad-boy bouncer turned strip-club owner to everyone who knew me, caught in a full-on embrace with a high-end escort in the middle of South Beach. And it was the best I'd felt in months. Fucking months.

Lingering in Chantilly's embrace a second or two longer than appropriate, I finally said, "All good, babe. All good," before releasing the woman from my arms, feeling empty as soon as I did. She was all I had . . . my only true connection to the woman I really wanted, Lynx, was a five-foot-nine-inch bottle blonde with a tube of KY and a box of condoms in her small purse.

Chantilly hooked her hands on her hips. "Come on, Mikey, don't play games with me. You good? Business booming at your joint?"

I smiled. "Yeah, business is always booming. Got good girls who make even better money. You should come work for me. Got a girl who'll show you the ropes, help you make a decent living."

She laughed. "Nah, baby. I got a good gig. Heading over to the upscale joint on Seventeenth now for a big-money job. Don't you worry about me, honey."

I tilted my head toward the sidewalk. "Come on, I'll walk you."

She hooked her arm in mine as we walked slowly.

"Did you have some extra free time and decide to take a walk on the wild side tonight, Mikey, or you here for your regular?" Chantilly asked as we made our way to her destination.

"The usual."

The call girl stopped and turned to face me. "Michael, honey, I haven't seen her. She's gone. Haven't seen her in thirteen months. Told you she was cagey the last time I laid eyes on her, was up to something she knew I wouldn't like. A gig even I wouldn't be down with, so she clammed up. I'm worried just like you, but there's nothing we can do." Placing a hand on my arm, she said, "This isn't something we can involve the authorities in, honey. We gotta let it go."

Michael.

tinged

God, it's been so long since a woman called me by my full name. One woman specifically.

Arriving at the entrance to the Fritz Hotel, I lied when I said, "I know," before letting her go do her thing. I might not have approved of what she was about to do, but Chantilly was her own woman. And I knew better than anyone, when a woman was an escort, there was little to nothing anyone could do to change her mind.

I figured it was a mindset so deeply ingrained, a facade any self-respecting girl immersed herself into in order to degrade herself enough to hook, it took nothing short of a military de-conditioning like in the Special Forces.

Watching the last person known to have seen Lynx on the Florida Coast walk away from me, resigned to let the whole situation drop, I knew what I had to do. Call Carson. It was something I'd been avoiding, but the problem was too big for me. I needed his help, and quick. Women didn't just up and disappear without a trace.

I walked back with a full-blown knot in my stomach and slipped into my white BMW. Before I sped out, I flicked my finger against the green dice hanging from the rearview mirror, watching them rock back and forth in limbo, just like my life. I brought those dice all the way from Sin City with me. Funny, my life had been hanging by a thread since I left there two years ago.

Palm trees fluttered in the breeze along Collins Avenue as I cruised along, hoping for a glimpse of long, lush pale brown limbs, and not really seeing anything else. I tried to appreciate some of the beauty surrounding me, but I couldn't, because the most beautiful gem I'd ever known was gone.

Gone.

two

SCRUBBING A hand over my face, I rolled over and picked up my phone to look at the time. It was early, just seven in the morning on Monday, my day off.

Lying back down, I dragged the small, lithe figure still snuggled next to me even closer. My dick rubbed against her ass as I ran my hand along her side and moved her hair out of the way so I could kiss her neck. She moaned softly, a small, yet eager sound floating from her lips. It drifted along all my senses, brightening my day, making my entire body pop awake at the promise she was making without a word.

The woman made good on it throughout the day, following through with her unspoken promises from the morning. After all, it was supposed to be my day of relaxation, and lately, the only way I relaxed was with a good fucking.

I was certain that would catch up with me eventually—like the bottle of JD cradled in my hand. I'd turned into someone I barely recognized.

Oh, wait. I did a little. I was becoming an even more despicable version of my manwhore dick of a father.

tinged

SLIGHTLY HUNG over from my pity party for one, I brushed one hand over my fresh buzz cut and yanked open the side door to the Wave with the other, allowing the bright Miami sunlight to blare inside the cool, light purple ambience of the club. It was Tuesday, and the girls were having a planning meeting backstage with Petal, now back to her birth name, Staci. She was another girl in a long line of Asher's rescue projects.

Now I was tasked with turning Staci into a legitimate businesswoman, if that was what you called a woman with nothing more than a GED who'd started out lap dancing at Sin City's finest adult establishment and was currently training to take over the Wave, Miami's steamiest adults-only nightspot. It wasn't exactly what one would label as success—until you took into account where the girl came from and where she was headed now.

If not for the Electric Tunnel, Staci might be whoring herself out to some fat, sweaty fuck with a small dick—like Lynx did, does, or whatever—so I'd say it was a big fucking whopper of a success.

And just like that, my mind was no longer focused on my business day, but tortured again with worry about the girl I couldn't forget or let go of. *Motherfucker.*

"Hey, Big Mikey," Marta called out to me with a smile, drawing me out of my fog and dragging me unwillingly back to the present.

"Hey, darling," I said, giving her a chin lift. She'd left my bed less than twenty hours ago. I owed her a decent hello, at the very least.

The beautiful specimen in front of me was the first girl I discovered in Florida. I met her at the hotel pool when I was here scouting locations for the Wave, and decided to bring her in to dance when she solicited me to hire her as an escort.

Asher warned me not to sleep with her, but I couldn't fucking listen to my friend, mentor, former boss, and current partner. As if he really knew shit about relationships. The dude had messed up the first decade of his own kid's life while hitting up every easy lay in Vegas, stringing along a good woman who loved him.

But this girl Marta was incredibly hot, all curvy and exotic with dark Mediterranean tanned skin, more like rich, black Mexican coffee than café au lait, contrasting with light blue eyes and long, flowing red-highlighted hair. She was soft and caring in a way I wasn't used to. None of the women in my life so far had treated me that way. Not my pill-popping mom, nor my bitch of an ex, Rochelle, who cheated on me with my dad. Or Lynx, the one woman who left me high and dry, holding my dick in her purse while she stomped my heart on the floor.

That's not being entirely fair. Lynx was gentle when she forgot she was supposed to be hard.

There was no way I could resist Marta's charms. I was so hard up, constantly worked up from seeing new and mysterious girls onstage, and she was so easygoing about the whole thing. The girl took what I gave her—a dinner here, a sleepover there, a day spent in bed once every week—and never asked for a damn thing more.

It was fun, sexy, easy, and absolutely nothing more. Zero emotions involved. *After a lifetime as Mr. Relationship, I'm that guy. Mr. Cold and Removed.*

Eh, I wasn't as tough as I made myself out to be. I cared for Marta. She just wasn't who I loved or obsessed over.

The outer club was mostly quiet as I headed toward the back. A slow R&B vibe floated through the main floor as I scanned the sparkly, scantily clad group gathered for the meeting.

"Hello, ladies. Y'all good?"

Yes, I'd adopted a little bit of a Southern twang in the last couple of years since ditching the desert.

Staci spoke for the whole gang of iridescent beauties. "All good, Mike. We have seventeen bachelor parties prebooked for this week, all of them complete with limo, booze service, and VIP treatment. I'm giving the ladies their assignments and working the dance rotations, so everything is fully covered and leaves flexibility in the schedule for walk-ins and other groups."

"Good. You got this, honey," I said before I slipped back to my office.

It wasn't upstairs like Asher's at the Tunnel, but it was just as tricked out. Private bathroom with shower, wet bar, leather couches, and a video feed of the entire the club were just a few of the features I'd had installed. I spent a lot of time there, mostly because I ran a tight fucking ship when it came to the club, and there was nothing I didn't have eyes on.

Or at least one eye, while the other scanned the window facing the streets of South Beach.

With my feet propped on my desk, my thoughts drifted to how the hell I ended up here permanently. Not here in Miami, but pining for a woman who clearly didn't give two shits about me.

In reality, it all started four years ago when Asher finally settled down with Natalie, and I started making monthly pilgrimages to muggy

tinged

Florida. Between helping Asher's pseudo-sister and best friend, Lila, build a new strip club in California while still running the bouncers and security at the Tunnel in Vegas, I spent wads of money and all my patience chasing after Lynx down here.

Of course, every goddamn trip ended with me on my knees, pleading with Lynx to come back to Vegas with me. I'd begged her to leave Bruno, her pimp. I'd tried to bargain with her to allow me to erase her debt. It was an endless, fruitless, vicious cycle in which I refused to give up and Lynx refused to surrender. There was some unknown grip Bruno had on her, and I needed to be closer to understand.

My gaze swept the room, taking in my office, looking around the four walls where I'd worked and sometimes slept for the better part of the last twenty-four months. It was more a home than my actual home.

Years back, when it had finally fucking dawned on me that I needed to be closer to the source to get what the hell Lynx was doing, I'd planted the seed for a Miami club in Asher's head. The Electric Cove in Los Angeles had been open for close to two years, and it was the hottest place on the West Coast. With Lila at the helm and Asher's Electric brand behind her, the Cove was the bomb.

So I did what any cock-blocked, warm-blooded man would do. I preyed on Asher's weakness—his ever-growing need to provide for his family, to create a legacy. He wanted to build an adults-only empire, and my personal plans jibed with that. He and I built the Electric Wave from the ground up, and I moved my sorry ass from the desert to the thumping streets of South Beach.

To be near her. To save her, or whatever the hell I thought I could do.

But things didn't go as planned.

Lynx was making crazy bank putting her goods on sale. So much so, she'd quit school entirely and was a hundred ten percent loyal to Bruno. Actually, more faithful to the greasy glorified pimp than me. That alone should have discouraged me, but like the lovesick fool I was, I didn't let it. I continued to hold out hope that her dream of getting a degree and her feelings for me would conquer all.

And then she left. Something I'd never expected to happen.

With that memory churning in my gut, I leaned my heavy head on my desk and swallowed back memories like bad tequila on an empty stomach . . .

BACK IN Vegas when I'd first met her as Lincoln, Lynx was still a jack-of-all-trades at least trying to be a student.

I'd first laid eyes on her at a party hosted by my old prep school buddy, Clay. I'd been a bit slow on the uptake that night, realizing a little too late that she wasn't another guest but had been hired to entertain for the evening.

And by entertain, I meant get down and dirty with whoever wanted her, however they wanted her. It was Vegas, and anything went.

Thinking back, it had been the best and worst night of my life. That evening, high on a balcony overlooking the Vegas Strip, I sealed my current fate.

Leaving Lincoln on the terrace, I forced her to promise she wouldn't go anywhere while I ran inside to grab some wine and one of the quilts from the beds. I'd run so fast through the enormous hotel suite, I broke out in a sweat. My palms were clammy at just the thought of a girl leaving before I got the chance to get to know her better. The way her amber-flecked eyes sparkled and her creamy coffee-colored skin reflected in the moonlight intrigued me before she'd uttered a word.

But there had been something else about her. Underneath all that radiance, there was pain. Something deep and unrequited. Not like the poor-little-rich-boy shit I had experienced. I could tell this woman—the one who told me her real name was actually Lynx—was broken.

And I was going to fix her.

It wasn't insta-love or any of that silly bullshit. I wasn't even sure I knew about love or what that word meant. But this girl sparked some deeper, dormant need deep inside my core.

I'd never understood Asher's rescue fantasy until that very moment.

After we got all the formalities out of the way, we settled onto the blanket. The Vegas skyline was our background, twinkling and sparkling, but it was nothing compared to when Lynx looked at me.

She leaned against my shoulder and we clinked glasses before we both said "jinx" at the same time.

"We should say Lynx," I teased her, and she giggled.

"This is kind of like being in a movie up here," she said. "It's so magical. Look at all the lights and traffic down there, and here we are sitting above it all. Reminds me of sitting on the Hollywood sign in high school."

"You did that?"

"Yep. It was a dare, and I was never one to back down from a challenge. So my friend Marie and I climbed right up on that sucker and watched the sunrise."

"Amazing," I said, taking all of Lynx in. Her smile, the roundness of her tits, the curve of her hips, and her long, lean legs spread out in front of her. She was gorgeous.

Leaning back a bit so I could concentrate on her face, I said, "Tell me about Lynx."

The sadness deepened in her eyes. Even in the dark, I could see them turn almost black.

"Not much to tell. Grew up in LA. My mom died a few years back from cervical cancer, and I moved here. Dad's been gone since I was two. Apparently, he liked his other family better. According to my mom, he went out to get a drink one night and never came back." She shook her head and changed the subject. "I'm putting myself through school. I'm at a branch campus of UNLV for fashion design. That's it."

I reached a semi-shaky hand across her face and pushed her long braids behind her ear. I was nervous as fuck all of a sudden. Yeah, I worked at the Tunnel, slumming it as a bouncer, but I'd never slummed it when it came to the ladies. I'd been raised on prep-school pussy and spent the last few years living with Rochelle, who only lasted that long because her honey was grade-A.

Apparently, my dad agreed where Rochelle was concerned.

"That can't be it. You're the most beautiful woman I've ever laid eyes on, and that's no line," I told Lynx.

She laughed. It was so soft and throaty, I wanted to grab it with my hand and keep it. I imagined it was a laugh just for me, and not one she would use when she was working a job.

Then she poked me in the shoulder and said, "You're funny."

"I'm serious. Actually, I'm a bouncer at a strip club, and I see women all the time . . . gorgeous women, and none of them compare to you."

This time, she didn't laugh or play-punch me. She blushed. A faint pink hue rushed across her bronze cheeks and neck, and my dick stirred in my jeans as warm blood pumped heavily through my veins. I took off my basketball warm-up jacket, leaving me feeling exposed in my black T-shirt, the tattoo running up my forearm on display. She peeked but didn't say anything.

Turning the tables on me, she said, "Tell me about you, Mike, other than that you spend your days and nights with gorgeous women."

I leaned against the wall behind me, pulling Lynx back against my chest, our legs tangled together, and pulled the blanket up over her shoulder. "Let's see. My name is Michael. Michael Anthony Wind, but everyone calls me Big Mike."

"I think I prefer Michael," she said confidently.

"You may be the first. Anyway, I was born and bred here in Vegas, raised with money and nannies, and I hated every second of it. I know . . . real first-world problems. My parents divorced a while back, and my mom never really bounced back. My dad keeps trading up for younger makes and models. And me, I skipped out on college and went to work as a bouncer. I guess you could say, I cashed out of their lifestyle a long time ago."

Lynx smiled, her lips turning up on both sides, her white teeth shining through. "Well, Big Mike, sounds to me like you got it all figured out. You didn't like where you came from, and you made a change."

There was no reason to mention my trust fund and the millions I had sitting in the bank, waiting for me to actually do something with my life. That knowledge always changed people's perception of me, and I liked being just a bouncer.

Her hand went to my arm and traced the letters inked there. "Now I know what this means."

CASH OUT was inked in cursive along my forearm. I decided a long time ago that all my family had was too much. Wanting for nothing made a person not give a fuck.

"God, LA. What a cesspool that place is, right?" I said, changing the subject.

"Yep. It's so crowded and full of smog, and we didn't live in the best neighborhood. My mom was white, but the whiter neighborhoods never really accepted me. I didn't get asked on play dates or sleepovers or any of that shit since I had a black dad, even though he was way out of the picture, so Mom moved us to a more ethnic area. Still, I couldn't wait to get the hell out. There was so much crime, and I hated going to sleep at night."

The flashing lights of the Strip flickered in the background, but weren't the least bit distracting from the honest beauty in front of me. My heart pounded, and my brain worked overtime trying to think of what to say. What would be substantial and meaningful enough for this woman?

"Is your mom buried there?" I didn't know where that question came from. It bothered me that they were geographically separated, even though her mom was dead.

She shook her head. "That's the only reason I didn't want to leave. My mom was a good person at heart, but she was dealt a bad hand. Over and over again."

I pulled Lynx even closer. "I'm sure she was a beauty inside and out to be your mother."

Lynx tilted her head—giving me an opening—and I kissed her. Our mouths came together like the Paris Hotel's hot-air balloon floating in the nighttime sky. It was if our mouths were meant to be together, one dark and the other light, and I didn't mean pigment. For the first time ever, I was the light, the yin to someone's yang.

My tongue explored the soft cavern of her mouth as she turned and leaned her small tits into my hard chest. Her body was half pressed into mine, but I craved more, so I nudged Lynx to roll over. She turned around and we were front to front. With her smaller frame resting on mine, the blanket pulled up over us, a tiny moan escaped her throat as I pressed my hardness against her.

I ran my hand up and down her back. She was wearing a tiny little triangle bikini top and low-rise jeans, making it easy for my already burning hand to further sear as it made its way up and down her smooth skin. As my hand continued to take laps up and down her spine, feeling her tiny hard nipples rub up against my chest, my fingers drifted into the waistband of her jeans, feeling her ass.

Fuck, it was tight and perfect. Like I said, I watched strippers all day and night. I'd certainly know.

We stayed like that until the sun came up. Me—Mike Wind—a beacon floating in the middle of her rough waters.

That is, until she got a text from her neighbor asking her to run over and pick up her kid.

As it turned out, the other way Lynx earned her money—as a nanny—was for Natalie and her kid we'd never met. Natalie stripped at the Tunnel, and had an on-again, off-again thing with our boss, Asher, but kept her personal life on tight lockdown from all of us at the club.

I had been fucking blown away when I learned all this after dropping Lynx off and meeting the kid that morning. Now I knew why Natalie kept her cards close to her chest. It only took one look to see he was Asher's. No denying our boss had fathered that fucking kid.

And just like that, I'd been destined to almost drown in a barrel of whiskey while trying to be a refuge for both Lynx and Asher.

Turned out, I had only able to provide shelter for my boss—not for my woman.

I HOISTED MY head from my desk, locked my memories down tight, then stood on my own two feet and trekked out of my office. I made my way back through the club to check on my other business before the Wave opened for the night.

Winking at Marta, I slipped out the back door into the oppressive Miami heat. But it was nowhere near as stifling as my own guilt.

three

"TALK TO me." I breathed heavily into my phone as I shortened my stride, rolling my neck back and forth to allow the tension to drain from me.

"You okay, man?" Carson asked. "Did I catch you in the middle of something?"

"Just taking a run, blowing off steam. It's a little early for you, isn't it?" I glanced at my watch, coming to a full stop.

"I'm working a case up in Philly, staying at my old place, so I'm on Eastern time. Every goddamn time I come back, I think I'll love batching it for a few days, but it actually sucks. That's why I'm freaking awake and thinking about how I gotta help you find a slice of the happiness pie, Mike."

"Yeah, yeah. What the hell you got for me, Carson?"

I'd been running for over an hour. My lungs and legs were burning, and I needed a break. With the early morning Saturday sunrise gliding upward and strengthening, the golden glow beating down on my scalp and sweat dripping down my neck, I plopped down on one of the benches lining the beach pathway.

Carson chuckled. "A little early for you to be breaking a sweat unless you're in bed, isn't it?"

The tide was coming in, but I could barely hear the waves crashing over my own racing heartbeat. And it wasn't the run that was making it speed up.

"Not now, man, cut the crap. I'm batshit tired. Haven't been sleeping, and I got to work the tension off somehow. Tell me, do you have anything for me?" I asked him again, straightening my legs in front of me, shaking them out.

"A whole lot of bullshit, my friend. Her social's right, matches up with her full name, Lynx Whisper Bennett. You got all that right in your snooping. Shows Nat's old apartment down in Florida as her last residence. Also shows her living in Vegas before that with Trish, next door to Nat. Before that, everything is a bit foggy. Her mom moved a lot, didn't always register her for school. Looks like Mom worked a bunch of cash-only jobs. Lynx's connection with Natalie is the most consistent piece of information, other than one private cell number she kept in frequent contact with down there. Area code is 305, so Miami."

"Fuck *before*, Carson. The number's probably her pimp. Give me what happened *after*, after she left Miami, and where the hell she went, dude."

I shouldn't be a dick since he was the only friend willing to help me. As an ex-FBI agent, Carson was putting his neck on the line for me, and I was trying to control how deeply he got involved. I wasn't sure how far his wife, Lila, was going to support me in this game of hide-and-seek, but I needed to find Lynx like I needed a shower.

Badly.

"Well, that's the part that's all wrapped up nice and tight in bureaucratic red tape, my man. The after."

"What the fuck?" I slammed my hand into the bench, the impact reverberating through my bones.

"My guy says *no way*. He doesn't have clearance to access the information, and he's got elevated status. Somebody pretty damn high up has shit sealed tight. I'm going to have to keep climbing the ladder and doling out chits, but it's no problem. I know who to ask. I got this."

"Shit, I didn't mean to rope you in like this." I sighed, regret joining the sweat seeping from my pores.

Carson's voice hardened. "Mike, did you keep Lila safe when no one else did? You nodding? Right, so shut your trap. I'm going to do every fucking thing I can."

The sound of a motorcycle turning over came through the phone.

"Sounds like you do enjoy parts of being alone in Philly. Taking a ride?" I ran a hand over my forehead and behind my head, sending beads of sweat flying.

I could be happy for my friend. I wasn't that fucking callous.

"Ha! Don't say anything. I got a little time and thought I'd take advantage of it. Don't mention it to Lila, okay? She's got enough pregnancy hormones running through her as it is."

"Of course," I said, assuring him his secret was safe with me.

I stood and paced around the narrow bench, unable to control the emotions twisting and turning through my veins. I could have probably run another seven or eight miles just to burn off my tension, but I had to get back home. To the warm body in my bed, even though my head and heart were with another woman who was turning out to be a ghost.

God, I'm messed up. A rat-fucking bastard.

"Look, I know you feel indebted to me, or some shit like that," I said to Carson. "But don't let Lila get upset over this. You got a wife and kid now, man, and another one on the way. They got to come first."

I took in the vacant lot in front of me, the sun casting a faint orange tinge on the debris, and also casting shadows on a pipe dream of mine . . . a dream Asher and I shared. We had bulldozed the old piece-of-crap building that had been here to make room for our new boutique hotel—all part of my plan to make myself a decent man.

An honorable, stand-up man worthy of Lynx when I get her back.

Carson's voice turned serious. "Dude, I know what I'm doing. We're going to find her and bring her back. Okay?"

"Yeah." I turned and headed back toward the bay and the high-rise condo I kept near the club.

"Later."

"Thanks, Carson. I mean it."

As I stepped back into my bachelor pad, the frigid air-conditioning joined the smell of bacon to slap me in the face. Shit, Marta was up, and I still had to talk with Asher about a few issues with the new hotel. And I really needed some time alone to digest my call with Carson.

Asher had gifted me the house he owned here in Miami. A big-as-fuck mansion, all decorated and shit, but I chose to punish myself in this barren stainless apartment close to the beach. It kept my mind focused and alert, and gave me a vantage point to keep scanning the streets. If I wasn't staring out the window of my office, I was gazing off the balcony of my condo.

"Morning!" rang out from the kitchen.

I mentally counted back three hours. Five o'clock in the morning out in Vegas, which was a little later than we usually touched base on this project. Natalie didn't know about the venture yet, which I didn't think was a good idea, but it was Asher's choice, not mine.

What the fuck did I know about having a wife and kids? *Nothing.* So I kept my mouth shut.

"Hey, Mart." I wound my sweaty arms around her from behind. "Smells good," I mumbled in her ear as I leaned forward and kissed the lobe.

"Better than you." She laughed, moving to turn the bacon and crack a few eggs.

"Yeah, I'm going to hit the shower real quick, but I have to call Ash first," I said, moving toward the master bedroom.

"Okay. I'll wait to put on your egg whites," she called after me.

Crap. Marta was so easygoing and accepting, and I was going to break her heart one day soon. More proof my reckless fucking around was going to catch up with me. Hopefully, really soon, now that Carson was involved.

Truth be told, I cared for Marta. If it hadn't been for my inability to let the past go, we might have been able to have something together. She was a good girl, and I was falling for her.

She was all legs, soft and supple curves, and dark, luscious tits. Deep down, I knew her heart was golden, but she knew when to be tough. None of the VIPs at the club got away with shit when they were in the back with her. She'd put them right in their place with a look and a waggle of her finger.

But my memories wouldn't allow me to go all-in with the exotic beauty. And she didn't ask. She knew better.

I hoped.

After my call, I stepped into a steaming shower, leaned my forehead against the cool tile, and closed my eyes as the water beat down my back. Asher had asked me to do the one thing I didn't want to do.

"I need someone to come and keep an eye on the Tunnel while I take the fam away, Mike. Pete's looking after Los Angeles and you got Staci out there, and I really need this. That okay with you?" he'd asked toward the end of our call.

I'd said "of course" without hesitation. In a million years, I'd never say no to Asher. He was the only one who had ever given me the acceptance and devotion I'd needed when all I'd been was a down-and-out spoiled teen looking for a place to call home.

But I hadn't been back in Vegas in a while. I'd been in and out a few times for my dad's birthday and Asher's wedding, but those were quick trips.

Asher and Natalie and Carson and Lila were taking all their kids to the Bahamas for a week, which meant I needed to really get down and dirty in Sin City. I wasn't sure why it bothered me so much. Lynx wasn't in Vegas, but it was where we'd met and started whatever it was that we had.

Which currently was a big fat nothing.

Running my hand over my short hair, letting the water wash away the sweat and dirt, I allowed my hand to roam. With Marta right there in the kitchen, I should have been ashamed of what I was doing, but I wasn't. Not with Vegas looming. The city of sin for most, yet the place I discovered the purest, most beautiful soul.

My thoughts drifted to my old condo. Lynx had been determined to keep paying for her schooling and was hooking in order to do that. I didn't like it, but what else could I do? It wasn't my place to force her hand. Natalie didn't know about us, so Lynx had also kept her apartment next door to Nat for appearance's sake. All these charades cut into her funds.

I should have told her about my trust fund and paid for her schooling, but somehow, I knew that wouldn't fly. So I took what I could get. And that was Lynx hanging out at my place when she wasn't selling her body or babysitting. It was a half-baked arrangement, but I couldn't afford to be picky.

My cock hardened at the memory of Lynx naked in my condo, walking to the bathroom to shower, her long braids swaying against her ass, then getting dressed in silky lingerie—inevitably, for someone else.

My mind floated back to one night when she was leaning against the floor-to-ceiling windows, her hands pressed against the glass and mine tight over hers, locking them in place, and my cock buried deep in her ass.

Squeezing myself hard before skimming up and down my shaft, I remembered that moment with precise clarity. I'd been watching Lynx's reflection in the glass, her tits bouncing free while her tight light brown nipples pushed up against the window. No one could see in, but we could see out. The twinkling lights of the Strip spread out in front of us, reflecting off our arms and legs, casting a soft glow around the room.

The city I'd grown up in was there for the taking, glowing like a beacon as it waited for me to conquer it. Vegas was my town, and it was on her streets that I'd learned to be a man. With Lynx in my condo, I'd envisioned for the first time building an empire of my own. My dad wouldn't be the only Wind to put up hotels and amass a fortune. I could do it too.

It wasn't just the sex that made me confident. Being with Lynx brought out something primal in me. I was king of the jungle, ready to attack my prey and carry the prize back to my mate.

And the sex was freaking awesome.

Even now—as nothing but a memory—Lynx's tight pussy, her round ass, and the way she didn't leave anything on the table made my heart race and my dick surge in my hand.

Any misgivings she'd had about me slumming it with her had been pushed to the side. It didn't matter that we were from two different worlds. Like me, she didn't have any inhibitions, and we'd had the best fucking sex I'd ever had. Dirty, kinky, freaky, slow, sensual—I'd loved it all.

I picked up the pace, roughening my grip as my balls tightened under me, ready to explode as I pictured running my fingers over her soft skin. My calloused hand had traveled slowly, brushing the side of her breast, lingering near her nipple that was peaking and pointing, before finding its way to her clit.

My hand worked overtime on my cock as I remembered strumming her clit while the tip of my dick breached her ass. God, it had been fucking tight like a vise. I remembered feeling like I'd died and gone to heaven, and wanted to stay there forever.

"I'm coming, Michael," Lynx had moaned, biting into my other hand that still held hers in place on the window.

Michael. She'd been the only one to ever call me that, mostly when we were in bed or making love. It was charged with a feeling I'd never associated with myself, even during all those years I'd lived with my high school sweetheart, Rochelle. Lynx's mouth said *Michael,* but her words breathed love.

That evening, her voice had been hoarse and throaty, and at her words, I'd gone over the edge. I slammed into her, pumping in and out until my cum dripped out of her.

"Shit!" I yelled in the shower as I tugged my hand up and down,

tinged

coming while leaning my head against the tile—a little too hard.

With a heavy dose of remorse weighing me down, I got the hell out of the shower and toweled off before heading out to eat bacon and eggs . . . with the woman who currently warmed my bed.

four

Two weeks later

WHEN I landed in Sin City, the sun was starting to set and the lights had come on over the Strip. Throwing my duffel over my shoulder, I walked outside and breathed in the early evening desert air. It was the same dry, scratchy stuff I'd grown up on, and it settled my lungs as much as it kicked up my nerves.

Spotting the Tunnel's pimped-out SUV, I threw a peace sign up in the air with two fingers before whistling to get Billy's attention.

"Hey, man." His blue eyes twinkled at me as I jumped into the passenger seat of my old ride and tossed my shit behind me.

"What's up, Billy boy?"

He huffed as he looked over his shoulder and pulled out. "I just left a warm Sadie back in my bed to come and get your sorry ass."

"Tough shit!" I smirked, thinking I called that relationship when Billy was still wet behind the ears and screwing up his security detail at the Tunnel. Knowing Asher, he'd be setting Billy and Sadie up with their own club before they even knew what was happening.

"I know, I know! It's not often that we get the prodigal son back here."

"Hey, we're all Asher's prodigals. He just keeps moving us out and setting up another of us as top dog."

Billy snorted. "You got his number. Rumor has it, he's shipping Sadie and me off to either Seattle or Texas when he gets back from the Bahamas. Apparently, Petey's got some guy under him in Los Angeles that's coming here to take my post."

"Sounds about right. It's been a few years since I left, so it's your turn to move on. Hold up—can you swing by my condo, and then we can go directly to the club?" I asked, keeping my gaze firmly on the road in front of me.

Billy flicked a glance at me before returning his attention to the road. "You don't want to unwind a little? I thought I'd just drop you at the condo and send someone to grab you later."

"No."

"Come on, Mikey, you've got to let that shit go. It's been four years since you fell for her. All you've done is mope and beg that chick to do one single fucking thing for you. I know you cared for her and you got memories and all that crap, but from what Asher says, she's in the wind. Like I said, let it go."

Slamming my hand on the dash, I turned to face my friend. "She's not in the fucking wind. She'll be back, and I'm going to find her first, Billy. She deserves that, just like everyone else in our gang. Thank fuck we loved Sienna when she told us about her past as Lila. And the way we took Quinn under our wing when we learned Asher was his father? Or the way we accepted Petey into the fold, even though he lied about being Asher's half brother? We're a fucking family, and I want my girl."

Billy held up a hand. "I got you, man. I hear you loud and clear. Believe me, we want you to find her. But all that doesn't mean you can't chill at your condo for a while."

"It does," I said as he pulled into my condo's garage. I kept the place just in case Lynx came back there looking for me. The doorman knew to let me know if anyone—particularly Lynx—stopped by. The money didn't mean a damn thing to me. I would never sell it until she was back for good.

"Keep the motor running, I'll be right back down," I told him as I slammed the passenger door.

I ran upstairs and grabbed my pistol out of the safe, shoving it in the back of my jeans and covering it with my track jacket. I threw my bag on the couch but quickly snagged it back up—I didn't have any intention of staying at the condo full of memories. I could sleep in Asher's office if I wanted to—as soon as he got the hell out of Dodge tomorrow.

Jumping back into the SUV, I yelled, "Let's go, Billy. Time to make some money and take care of the ladies on the stage!"

Inside the Electric Tunnel, I felt almost normal. Taking one deep breath after another of the crisp oxygenated air, I was home. I loved it there. And I adored Asher more than my own father, even though Asher thought I should let go of Lynx.

He didn't get it. Nat had literally fallen back into his life. Yeah, he had to work for it, but he knew where the fuck she was.

Some song about *twerking it* blared through the speakers as I roamed the floor, slapping all the bouncers on the back, and kissing all the lovely women wearing thongs and G-strings. The navy-blue walls were like a balm to my battered heart. This pulsing deep-purple haze of a place was my home.

Sydney Luv kissed my cheek when I walked up to the back bar. "Hey, Big Mike."

Sydney was an all-American beauty. All creamy freckled skin and strawberry-blond locks, she was an angel—an angel who did a damn good job of stripping. But she wasn't really my type. Over the last few years, my preferences ran darker. Not just sexually, but skin color too.

The dancers had been trying to get me to break down and sleep with one of them for years. *Not gonna happen.* If they knew I was screwing one of my dancers in Florida—with regularity—they would fucking shit.

"Hey, baby," I said, playfully smacking her ass peeking out from neon-green hot pants. "How's it going, honey?"

"All good. I bought a new place over in Summerlin, and I'm sharing Sienna's old slot with Sadie. Although, Billy's losing patience. He wants Sadie off the stage," she said, swirling her tongue around a cherry from her amaretto sour, still trying to tempt me.

I was pretty sure they had a bet going in the dressing room. First one to fuck Big Mike got a thousand bucks.

"My guess is that's gonna be happening real soon, little girl." I motioned for the bartender, completely unaffected by the stunning half-naked woman, and ordered, "Jack, neat."

The drink was in my hand before I could take another breath. I ran the tumbler under my nose, inhaling the barrel-aged oaky scent before tossing the drink back. Then I went to find Asher, pretty sure he was eager to head home to his wife.

tinged

And he was. I found him up in his office, counting cash and shoving it in the safe.

"Honey, I'm home," I said, banging open the door.

At nearly forty years old, Asher didn't even flinch. He just grabbed a pistol from his drawer and pointed it with perfect aim at my heart.

"You asshole. You're gonna get yourself killed, Mike." He tucked it back in the drawer before he stood and came my way, gathering me in a bro hug.

"Nah, I'm just as quick," I said, whipping out my own piece.

I remembered a time not too long ago when things weren't so playful between Asher and his pistol and me. Natalie had fled to Miami, and Asher had just learned he was the one who had knocked her up during an ugly threesome. I hadn't wanted to tell Asher where she was, but when he shoved a gun at my temple, I didn't have much of a choice.

That was when Lynx packed up to help Natalie and never came back.

And I fell in love with a quart or ten of Jack Daniels.

"Put your gun down, Mike. My wife is waiting for me to get home and fuck her."

Settled back in his chair with his boots up on the desk and his wild blond hair sticking up in every direction, Asher asked, "What's up with our hotel?"

I sat opposite him, propping my basketball shoes up on the desk too. "Foundation going in this month. Permits are all set. The plans have been approved all around. Thirty luxury one-bedroom suites and fifteen two-bedrooms, a lounge, high-end restaurant, and coffee shop all ready to be put up in one of South Beach's premier blocks. As soon as the whole thing is framed, the work on the lap pool and decks overlooking the ocean will start. Maybe ten, twelve months, tops."

"Good, I'm gonna tell Nat on this trip. We're getting a sitter down there and will have some time alone. She's probably gonna blow a gasket at first. But I got the plans on my phone and once she sees those, she'll be all in." He pulled his feet down and leaned forward. "You doing okay? Staci working out?"

"I'm fine, Ash. Staci is great and doing fine. She's ready to take over the whole place."

"I mean, are you doing okay, Mike? I know you're looking for Lynx and tapping that other piece of ass at the same time. Granted, I'm not one to judge, but you gotta either stop looking for Lynx or you need to make a go of it with the stripper. Not both."

25

I frowned, running a hand over the back of my head. "It's not like that. Marta likes us being casual."

Asher barked out a laugh. "Huh-uh. No woman likes casual, Mike, take it from me. She's waiting for you to forget about Lynx, and she's gonna be done waiting soon. Remember, she works for you. You're setting yourself up for a big mess." He leaned back in his chair and glared at me, his silver eyes shooting daggers my way.

"I can't believe it! Asher, the king of the threesomes, giving me relationship advice." I stood to go, but added, "I got it, Ash. I know what I'm doing. I got the club here while you're gone, and I got the hotel in Florida when I head back. And I got Staci, and I'm gonna find Lynx. Because I'm that fucking amazing, man."

"I'll be there in a heartbeat when you realize you're not that fucking amazing, Mikey-boy," Asher called after me as I strode out of his office at the top of his adult-entertainment empire. "And send me the reports from tonight to my phone!"

five

M Y FIRST two days in the desert went as planned. I spent most of my time taking care of the Tunnel. When I wasn't there, I hung out with a bunch of my old bartender buddies on the strip—staying out of the Palace where I met her—and successfully avoided being at the condo.

It wasn't until the third morning I was there and sleeping on Asher's new office couch that shit went sour. There I was, happy as fuck sleeping, thrilled that after Asher married Nat, he replaced the cesspool of semen and bodily fluids that he used to call a couch, when my phone buzzed with unwanted news.

Marta: Hey, baby! How you doing?

I sat up and stared at the screen, rubbing my hand over my face.

Mike: It's four a.m. here, seven where you are. What are you doing up?
Marta: I couldn't sleep. Miss you.
Mike: Don't get like that. I'll be back. I miss you too.

Marta: I know. I'm not wailing or anything. Just miss seeing you in general. Knowing you're okay.
Mike: I'm good, baby.
Marta: Hey, good news! Staci kicked me off this week's schedule so I could come out and be with you.

That goddamn Staci. What the fuck?

I stood and carried my phone to the bathroom, setting it on the counter while I drained the dragon. I didn't respond until I finished, kicking my foot up to flush.

Why did everyone in my life feel like they had to wade in and solve shit? Did Staci think I couldn't handle Vegas on my own? Or did she believe Lynx was never coming back? Even worse, had she convinced herself that Marta and I were a thing?

Mike: Baby girl, you don't have to do that. I'm good.
Marta: I got a flight. I'm leaving in a few. I'll text you when I'm there. Will you send someone? It will be during setup for the club.
Mike: Shit, I'll come myself. But you don't have to do this.
Marta: I know. I want to. And I've never been to Vegas before!
Mike: OK, baby.
Marta: See you soon!!!

My first thought was, *Where the fuck are we going to stay?*

In my crazed state of confusion, the black-and-white office spun until it looked gray. I decided to go on a run before it got too hot, but mostly to get rid of the craziness coursing through my whole body.

I didn't need this. All I wanted was to get the hell in and out of this town. Now I had to play fucking tour guide for Marta.

Don't get me wrong . . . I wanted to show her a good time. Anywhere but here.

She knew about Lynx and that I looked for her. But she thought it was out of some benevolence of my heart, that I didn't want some helpless woman on the street. Because in Marta's mind, I was compassionate and caring, not pining for what once was or could have been.

tinged

Marta came running out to baggage claim and flung herself into my arms, wrapping her legs around me. "Vegas, baby! Where anything can happen!"

I patted her on her tight ass and set her down before I kissed her. Closed mouth, but it was pretty fucking hot and held lots of promise. My dick perked up right away at the thought of this little visit, even if my other head wasn't in a good place.

"Hey, Mart. You got bags?" I grabbed her hand and walked toward the carousels.

"Duh. A few," she said, squeezing my hand.

A few minutes later with two suitcases in hand, we loaded up the Tunnel's SUV and headed out to either pure heaven or hell, depending on how you looked at it. Pulling away from the airport, I didn't even think twice before driving straight to one of my dad's hotels.

"Where's your place?" Marta asked as I parked the truck in front of the Luxious, the most luxurious of all his properties.

"It's down at the other end of the strip," I said, nodding in that direction. "But I thought we would make this more of a vacation."

I went to open the door but wasn't fast enough. She reached over the console and turned my face toward her. With her light blue eyes staring directly into my brown ones, she asked, "Is this okay?"

I turned my head, trying to wrestle free of her gaze. "Mart, come on. Don't do this here."

The valet attendants could apparently see we were having a tense moment. They gave us our space and didn't approach the vehicle as her eyes filled with tears.

Shit.

"Look, I know we're just fun and easy," she said, her voice cracking. "I get it. That doesn't mean that I don't care about you, Michael."

Hesitating, I pulled in a breath. The car felt stifling hot, despite the fact I'd just turned off the air-conditioning and the engine.

"Mike," I said, correcting her, then jabbed her with my elbow and winked. "Big Mike, baby."

Of course I was intentionally killing the moment. Marta was trying to be real and sentimental at the same time, but I couldn't do it. Especially when she called me Michael.

"Come on, darling, let's go have some fun. Yeah?" *As if either of us has a choice at this point.*

She sucked back her unshed tears and took a deep breath. "Totally." When she threw open her door and unfolded her long, lean stripper legs out of the vehicle, I noticed the guys were taking her in. They knew I didn't fuck my girls. Or at least, I didn't when I lived in Vegas. So, in their twisted minds, Marta was a free agent.

Alex approached. "Hey, Mike." When I tossed him the keys with a chin nod, he asked, "Want it up front?"

"Yeah, for now. We're checking in, so I'll be in and out for a few days."

Tossing my arm around Marta, I led her into the hotel. Fuck them if they thought they were going to even look at my lady.

As we stepped inside, not only did the sound of slot machines dinging slap me in the face, but so did the irony, and the realization of what a fucking prick I was.

Why the fuck did Asher have to be right?

SIX

Lynx opened the door to her apartment, smiling as she beckoned her visitor inside.

"Hello, Ms. Lincoln. I here for treatment today," the woman said in broken English.

"Yes, Sari, come in," Lynx said, closing the heavy door behind her.

"We go to your room." Sari headed toward the back of the apartment, lugging a folded table behind her.

"Let me help you," Lynx offered.

"No! You must not. This not your job," Sari said firmly, shaking her head.

Resigned, Lynx led the woman to her bedroom, decorated in varying shades of pink and gold. Small candelabra lights were lit above her bed, casting a soft glow on the satiny rose-colored bedspread and the deep cranberry fabric-covered walls.

Sari plugged in the canister of already warm wax, reheating it quickly while setting up the table. The tiny brown-skinned woman spread a long blue blanket on top of the table and plugged that in also so the sterile surface would be more comfortable for Lynx.

One long window was open a crack, allowing a hint of the sea breeze to waft inside, reminding Lynx of other happier oceans. She inhaled deeply, the salty tang calming her as she undressed with no shame. She didn't wear a bra, so she slipped off her red thong and climbed onto the semi-warm table.

She lay on her stomach first, baring her new tattoo, a series of purple-tinted waves cresting across her lower back. It had only been a few weeks since she'd had it done overseas, but thankfully, it wasn't tender anymore. With Sari's visit, she knew she'd have no room to complain in the coming days.

"Interesting," Sari said, running a finger along the tat. "Has Mr. Zayid seen this?"

The woman might be small, but she wasn't stupid.

"Yes, he sent the men with me when I had it done."

There was nothing to hide, except for the inscription hidden deep within the rolling water. Inside the finely detailed design on her darker skin were the words CASH OUT. So small, most likely unable to be seen by the naked eye, the tattoo artist had to use a magnifying glass when he inserted them.

"Okay, hold your cheeks, spread them," Sari instructed.

Lynx reached back and grabbed her own ass cheeks, opening them so the woman could coat her lower lips and ass crack with an apricot-scented hard wax. Lynx preferred the sea smell to the fruity scent, and her nose searched for the tranquility of the ocean air she so desperately needed.

Then she felt Sari fanning her ass, hastening the drying of the wax before pulling it off with no mercy. A few more tugs and pulls and she heard, "Turn over."

And she did, automatically bending her knees to the side and letting them fall flat, leaving her spread wide open. Sari didn't talk anymore, just diligently cleaned up Lynx's crotch, ripping the patches of hair that had grown in and plucking any loose hairs left behind until she was as smooth as the day she was born.

The scent of lavender filled the room as Sari wiped a soothing antiseptic over Lynx's now well-groomed most intimate parts, ready for visitors. Grabbing her hands, the little brown woman ran the same healing tonic over Lynx's palms, privy to the damage Lynx had inflicted there.

Closing her eyes and willing herself to relax, Lynx continued to lie still, her only movement straightening her legs. She knew what was coming last, but not least. Her thoughts went back to her tattoo as she felt a quick pinch in her arm. After two deep breaths, the sting of her birth-control injection faded. Sari lifted her other arm, tying the tourniquet tight above her elbow. Another prick, and Lynx felt the blood drain from her vein into the small glass vial.

She was required to stay clean, especially if she wanted to ever follow the words now inscribed on her skin. The simple words had come to mean so much to her. She was trying to cash out. But she couldn't just yet.

It wasn't just the insane access to money she'd grown accustomed to—she needed to do what she set out to do and find what she came for. Sadly, she hadn't done it yet.

"Okay, all done," Sari said, breaking Lynx from her thoughts.

Scooting off the table, Lynx wandered into the bathroom to clean up, and didn't come out until the other woman was long gone.

Not the right time to cash out yet.

seven

SINCE I'D left Vegas, I'd never really hit the Strip until this trip. Without daring to look back, I'd locked my piece up in Asher's safe before heading to Florida. With a firm bro hug and a kick on the ass with his motorcycle boot, Asher had sent me on my way two years ago.

Thank fuck.

After an hour of playing *Mr. Lucky and in Love in Vegas* with Marta and a week of being the big man in charge of Asher's empire, I wanted nothing more than a break. Some peace and fucking quiet.

And I desperately craved my window looking out onto the South Beach drag.

Showing Marta around should have been fun. But what started as a little nagging in my gut grew into a giant gaping abscess. I was stringing her along, and she knew it. Asher knew it. *And it only took twenty-four months for me to know it.*

The first night she was there was a disaster that ended in an even more noxious fucking.

After the scene at the valet station, we settled into an enormous suite at the Luxious. And for a moment, it appeared Marta forgot about her emotional outburst in the car. The room was the most outrageous place she'd ever seen.

Before we left to grab some dinner, she'd run around the place, smoothing her hand along the back of the silk sofa and sniffing at the votive candles filled with pomegranate-scented wax. I only knew the damn fucking smell because it was the signature scent in all of my dad's joints, compliments of his second wife.

Then Marta filled the Jacuzzi tub with bubbles and recreated the scene from *Pretty Woman* where Julia Roberts went from cheap streetwalker to kept woman in Richard Gere's penthouse suite. Watching her from the doorway to the bathroom—her ear buds in, swaying to music, most likely Matchbox 20 or something similar, with her eyes closed and her feet up on the ledge—my heart sank.

What the hell had happened to me?

I was chasing a hooker—one that I believed I was hopelessly in love with—and I was sleeping with my employee, who was a stripper. And I thought I'd hit rock bottom when Rochelle left me for my dad.

Locking my thoughts down tight, I took Marta out on the town. We ate sushi while overlooking the Strip, rode the elevator to the top of the fake Eiffel Tower, kissing at the top. That's where it got really fucked up. Because she grabbed my cock at the top, and I'm a dude, so I reacted.

It had been days since I'd unloaded myself. I certainly couldn't jerk off in Asher's office.

So, with half an erection, I took Marta back to the hotel and screwed her brains out before going to check on the Tunnel—leaving her behind to her *Pretty Woman* fantasies.

Before you get all judgy, I don't need any more guilt.

At first, I was lonely. Starting up with Marta was not only a dick move but also a kind of rescue fantasy. Now, I had no freaking clue what the fuck was up other than my heart belonged elsewhere. I needed to cut ties, even if it meant being alone for the rest of my life.

It wasn't until the next morning, when my phone rang while I was passed out on Asher's sofa, that I realized the enormity of my stupidity.

I had forgotten to go back to Marta at the hotel. Instead, I'd spent the wee hours of the night with a lowball glass and a bottle of JD.

With nowhere to turn or hide, I rushed back to the hotel with my tail between my legs and room service on the way. When I walked into the room, Marta gave me a kiss with a tight smile.

"I'm sorry I pushed you yesterday in the car," she said while sipping her orange juice.

The sweet citrus smell mixed with the scents of bacon and sausage, and when added to the generous helping of regret I'd walked in with, made my stomach and head spin like a giant industrial washing machine.

"It's got nothing to do with that, Marta. You know I'm fucked up in the head over her. And now I'm fucked up even more because of you."

A lone tear slid down her cheek, splashing onto her plate. I ran my hand along her face, slipping a few stray hairs behind her ear, and she closed her eyes. "I care for you, sweetie. I do. And you know in the last few years we've been together, I haven't strayed. Physically. Mentally, I could've never fully been yours."

"I know," she whispered. "I hoped and wished. Tried to keep it light and fun. But I still prayed you'd move on." She ducked her head, avoiding my eyes.

"I should've known. Paid better attention. I'm so stupid. I really thought you wanted fun. But then you knew how I took my eggs and showed up here, and I finally clued in." I raised her chin with my finger and cupped my hand on her cheek, taking in her sheer beauty. I was a fucking idiot, but I couldn't love her. Not like that.

"It's okay, Mike. I've known about Lynx since we first met. Not just the part about you looking endlessly for her and you cared for her, but that she was so much, much more to you. Remember she was there that first time you had me come by the club? She was up in your office when I arrived. I'd been there a few minutes. You'd been arguing, and I heard her screaming 'Never, no fucking way am I quitting.' When I heard you choking out 'I love you' through tears, my heart broke for you."

Breakfast long forgotten, Marta stood and went to look out the panoramic window. The reflection of her curves and her long eyelashes in the glass was stunning. Any man would be a downright fool to let that go.

And I was a fool. This gorgeous, caring woman would willingly walk through fire or do anything for me.

"I didn't know you heard us. But, yes, I remember her storming out as you walked in. It was one of a million fights we had, but it was the big one. The one where she totally dropped me, cut me off completely."

"I thought you were kind of adorable and sweet the first time I met you," Marta said, "but I could see in your eyes you were taken even back then. When I heard Lynx screaming in your office, I was a little happy. I thought maybe I could make you mine." A sob escaped Marta's throat as she leaned her forehead against the mirrored glass.

I came up behind her and ran my hand up and down her back, my rough fingers catching on her lace nightgown. "Shhh. Another time, another place, baby, and it would've happened. But I've been fucked up a long time over this, and I should've never started with you. You were irresistible," I said, placing a chaste kiss on the back of her neck.

She shook her head. "You were the irresistible one. And the one to get me off the streets, give me a good job, a decent one where I'm watched and protected. And I make amazing money."

Whiskey quietly seeped back up my throat like a slow-burning blaze. Why couldn't I convince Lynx to do that?

Marta turned and nodded once, not meeting my eyes. "I'm gonna go back home. This was a mistake, and I get it. It was all me. Don't you put this on yourself for a minute."

"Don't say that." I wrapped my arms around her, holding her tight—her back pressed into my front.

She broke free from my hold. "I hope you slay your dragons, Mike. I do. You deserve it." On her tiptoes, she reached up and kissed me on the cheek before walking to the bathroom and turning on the shower.

An hour later, I dropped Marta off at the airport and finished my time at the Tunnel.

eight

I'D BEEN back in Miami a week and the Wave was bumping. We were packed, just like we were every Saturday night. Rap alternated with heavy metal, pulsing through the rooms, and alcohol flowed freely at the bars. Our girls bared themselves freely, gyrating on the stage and on laps, making men and women alike very happy campers.

I'd just stepped out onto the floor after hiding in my office most of the night, but not from Marta. She was doing her thing, hanging upside down from a pole, her ankles twisted around the top, her tits mushed into the sleek silver metal, drawing the eyes of many men.

Thank Jesus she didn't bring our personal baggage into work.

I was hiding from my own shadow and what I might or might not do. My nerves were as frayed as the bottom of my running shoes. Although, I'd told Asher I could handle it all, the truth was I couldn't.

Not if I didn't find Lynx.

I was back to staying at Asher's old mansion where I could get lost in one of the cavernous rooms while I drank and cried myself into a stupor. The only one who would look for me there was Lynx. She knew the place from when Natalie was living in Miami with Quinn, and Asher came to stake his claim. He'd originally rented the joint, thinking he needed to set up camp permanently in Florida to be near his son. But after he made a life in Vegas with his family, he bought the property as a vacation rental.

A while later, he gave it to me to use, and now I wouldn't let him rent it. It remained a vacant beacon of hope, hopefully guiding Lynx back to me, just like my place in Vegas.

I'd just turned away from Marta's section and was heading to look in on the back of the bar when Sampson, my head bouncer, called me over the radio. He asked me to check on something at the main door for him.

"Be right there." I headed toward the front, passing turquoise leather banquettes set against lilac walls and rows of white snakeskin club chairs. Lila had picked out the decor, softening the signature navy and deep purple of the Electric brand with a more tropical vibe.

Hard to imagine she'd been a dancer once. Best there ever was after reinventing herself, narrowly escaping a brutal and violent marriage to some religious freak. Now she ran the most successful franchise of strip clubs with her best friend, Asher, and me.

And she was a mom.

Lila had been pregnant when decorating the Wave, and none of us were going to argue with a knocked-up ex-stripper. Turned out she knew what she was doing. This club had taken Miami by storm, and its popularity didn't seem to be letting up.

Good, because I needed the money to compensate Carson's guys when they came up with more information about Lynx.

"What the fuck?" I yelled when I finally reached the main entrance and took in the scene unfolding in front of me.

"We didn't know what to do, boss," Jovi said. In a lower voice, he added, "You always say no hookers."

"Get the hell out of my way, Jovi, can't you see this woman's hurt? Use your fucking brain instead of your ass!" Shoving him out of the way, I wrapped my arm around the high-priced call girl and walked her into the club. "Baby, what happened?"

Chantilly leaned her skinny frame into me. I could feel her shaking, tremors running through her entire body.

"Mikey, baby, they got me good," she said as I settled her on the couch in my office.

I took in her messy hair and torn skirt. *What the fuck?*

"Who?" I roared. "Who did this?"

Trying to force myself to calm down, I grabbed some ice from my bar and wrapped it in a soft towel. "Put it on your eye."

God, she's going to have one hell of a shiner.

"I don't want you doing anything stupid." She held the cold pack to her left eye as she shimmied out of her leather coat, revealing a huge bruise on her arm.

"Jesus Christ, Chantilly, just tell me who the hell did this!" I paced the small room, my Air Jordans pounding into the area rug, marking my path.

The hand holding the ice pack trembled. "I don't really know."

Taking a seat next to her, I took over holding the ice on her eye while taking one of her hands in mine. Running my thumb over hers, I said, "Shhh, I'm sorry. I'm trying to calm down. You need to take a deep breath and try to tell me as much as you remember."

Her chest rose and fell through a few deep breaths before she spoke. "Earlier today, I got a call from Bruno. He said there was a bigwig client rolling into town who was looking for a few new girls to entertain him and his friends. He told me they like kink, and a lot of it. Said they wanted two or three girls, a no-questions-asked kinda thing, but big money. Triple the usual rate." A shudder ran through her whole body.

I removed the ice and wrapped one arm tightly around her. "Shhh, you're doing good. Keep going."

Once she'd calmed herself somewhat, her words came again. "I got a daughter, Mike. I keep her dressed and fed. We go to the doctor and the dentist. Her dad's a deadbeat nobody and gives me shit. So, you gotta understand, I do what I do for her."

"Honey, I know. You don't have to justify anything to me," I said, smoothing my hand down her back and up again.

"So, I said yes. I told Bruno that it was no problem. For triple the pay, I could do kink." She lowered her gaze to the carpet.

I put a finger under her chin and raised her gaze to meet mine. "Don't, Chantilly. Don't beat yourself up."

"They wanted us at five o'clock, so I had my sitter take my girl to dinner while I got ready. I was gone by the time they got back. I was supposed to meet Trixie and Magnolia in the bar of the Fritz, and when we were all there, text Bruno for the room number and information. So, that's what I did. While we sat in the lounge having a cocktail, a bad feeling ran through me. Something felt off, but it was a big job. Who was I to complain?"

She stood and walked toward the bar, bracing herself against it but not looking at me. "We got the room number and headed up. It was the penthouse, of course, and as soon as we rang the buzzer, my stomach dropped. Everything felt wrong, especially when some foreign servant dude opened the door." She sucked in another big breath. "Can I take a drink?"

"Of course."

Pouring herself a few fingers of my Johnny Walker Black, she tossed it back like a pro. I watched her body still with the burn, afraid to move myself.

"It was a full-on mess when we walked in. Lines of coke on the table, four men sprawled on the sofas, music turned up loud, TVs on, A/C going full blast. Their shirts were open, and Trixie sighed at the sight of their muscled chests like she'd hit pay dirt. One of the guys on the couch stood up and welcomed us, then pointed toward the table. Trixie made for the table and snorted a line or two. He asked Magnolia and me if we wanted a drink, and we nodded. He asked if we wanted champagne, and we said sure."

Chantilly moved around my office, prowling mostly, seeming uncomfortable with her fresh bruises on display. She kicked off her heels and padded barefoot.

"By the time he got us our drinks, Trixie was already in the lap of one of the other men with her tits in his mouth and his hands down the back of her shorts. The first guy came back with our drinks and asked us to sit down. Said his name was Rahm and asked me my name, but wasn't interested in Mags and Trix at all. Then he put his hand on my knee and whispered in my ear that he'd put something in the drinks to make it all a little more fun. I didn't hesitate. I just tilted my glass over and poured it out on the carpet."

"Holy shit!" I jumped up and went to her, wrapping my arms around her and holding her tight. "You need to see a doc? You got something in your stomach?"

I wasn't even worried about the dudes at that moment, just Chantilly. Christ, she had a daughter. I didn't even know her name and where to find her if something happened to her mom.

"No, no. I'm fine. I didn't take that many sips before I drained the whole glass on the Oriental rug. I don't do drugs. Like I said, I got a daughter. But this dude, Rahm, went fucking ape-shit, Mike. Grabbed my arm and dragged me toward one of the bedrooms screaming, 'You'll not disrespect me, blondie bitch. I told your boss we have our way with the girls the way we want. And if I want to fuck your ass with my whole fist up your cunt while you're on X, then that is what I'm

41

doing.' I kept yelling for him to let me go, but he wouldn't."

"Jesus Christ, I need to talk with this Bruno." I let out a long breath. He needed to understand his girls were people, not pawns.

"It gets worse, Michael."

I wasn't sure what made my gut clench even more—her calling me Michael, or the part about it getting worse.

"When I tried to jerk loose, he screamed, 'That other cunt bitch wasn't into it at first either, but now little Miss Lincoln is quite happy with her arrangement.' And then he hauled off and sucker punched me."

The room spun, and I had to bend over and clutch my stomach. The few shots of whiskey I did earlier were coming back up, racing up my throat, accompanied by a scream.

"What else did he say?" I forced out, my words raspy.

Tears streamed down her cheeks. "Nothing. I ran. I'm sorry, Michael."

On the verge of a panic attack, I went to comfort the brutalized woman in my office. It wasn't her fault. I wanted to be mad that she didn't stay and ask more questions, get me something concrete. But it wasn't in me to be that way.

"Come on. Take a shower and get cleaned up," I told her. "We have to go see Bruno."

As I listened to the shrill sound of the shower pounding behind the closed bathroom door, I poured myself a stiff drink. Letting the amber liquid burn through my body, I prayed for it to relax me. It didn't.

I was drinking too much. After I found Lynx, I was going to cut back. The shit was barely taking the edge off these days. Then again, when I got my girl back, I wouldn't need alcohol.

Doubtful, but I was optimistic.

Grabbing my phone off the desk, I texted Carson.

Mike: I got info, my man.

Unable to sit still, I paced my little lair while I waited for a response.

Carson: Give me a minute, and I'm gonna call you.
Mike: Not now. Got one of Lynx's former coworkers in my office.

42

tinged

Carson: Oh man, don't go there.
Mike: Shut the fuck up. Not like that. She got the info.
Carson: Shit. Sorry.
Mike: Call me tomorrow. I'm going to see the pimp.
Carson: You sure that's smart?
Mike: No.

I tossed my phone back on the desk, not wanting to discuss my intentions with Carson. He threw all his ethics out the window when his woman was captured and held hostage in an underage hard-porn studio, and almost raped by her filthy excuse for an ex-husband. And I wouldn't do the same?

Damn right, I was going to see the pimp.

nine

AFTER APPLYING a depilatory to her legs, Lynx scrubbed herself clean in the shower. With all the hair removed from her body, she took time caring for her sensitive skin. Using a pumice stone to the inside of her palms, she removed any evidence of her desecrating her own skin. Then she sat on the settee near the window, rubbing coconut cream over her calves, smoothing it down her pedicured feet and back up to her flat tummy. She swirled it around the crystal stud in her navel, trying not to think about her past, present, or future. The last of which was so hazy, she could barely make out that one actually existed.

But it was hard not to drown in the sea of memories washing over her like a tsunami overtaking a small island.

Soft music played from the iPod dock in the corner, and an emerald off-the-shoulder Givenchy dress hung on the door. The song was sad to fit her mood. It was a melancholy tune with morose lyrics about missed chances and lost love. An electric violin struck a high note in the background, and Lynx let the wave of emotion sweep over her.

Missed chances in life and love—she knew about that. Like in her current situation, she missed the other girls she'd met here like a pup yearns for its littermates, long after they leave for their forever homes.

tinged

Lynx had been chosen as one of the favorites, which meant she was moved to her own apartment and was paid more to have sex less frequently. She went on trips to London and Singapore, and was the envy of all the other nameless faces and bodies who filled the group housing.

Yet she still yearned for the others. She missed their chatter and smiles, the movies and conversation they shared in the afternoons. Their words of comfort were all she had when she moved here.

She also had missed her chance to find what she came for, because the answers were buried somewhere deep inside that group of girls. And now she was rarely able to leave her little palace other than by *his* side.

Sighing, she slid the dress on over her silky skin, the green satin clinging to her curves. With her small breasts braless and free, the precious fabric rubbed her nipples, hardening them into tiny little peaks. There was nothing she could do about that. The sensation created by the silk reminded her of another man's warm breath and mouth, and her body reacted.

A man whose name she didn't dare breathe.

Her benefactor could never know any other man existed for her, or he would strike out against him. She was nothing more than a piece of property to her current man, but he didn't share well when it came to her. There was no way she could tip her hand, allowing him to see who her heart really belonged to.

Tonight, he would come, and Lynx would spread her legs and take him deep in her ass. She'd suck him in her mouth until he released all over her face. She would do whatever she had to because she was on a mission. For tonight, she planned to ask to visit the girls one afternoon. She'd say she wanted to show off her new swimsuit to the others.

As she stared at herself in the huge gilded mirror, Lynx could only think of the one man who truly cared for her.

"Michael," came out as a hushed whisper as she ran her manicured fingers down her cleavage and over her left breast, tweaking her own nipple. The dress hung loose off her shoulder as she worked herself up in preparation for the night ahead, pinching and squeezing her own breast until she was panting.

"Wonder what you're doing, baby? Are you happy? Do you miss me?" she said quietly to herself with her eyes closed tightly, imagining his face, his close-cropped hair soft and smooth like velour, and his strong frame. When he'd looked at her with all the compassion in the world, she'd always put up her shutters, keeping him and his love at bay.

Stepping back to sit on the bed, Lynx wrapped her arms around herself, pretending they were muscled and firm. The image of his tattoo floated in front of her still tightly closed eyes . . .

SHE AND Michael had been standing on the beach that day, her back to his front, his erection pressed against her ass. Her hair was unbraided and loose, flying around both their faces in the breeze.

The warm ocean air had been their cocoon, protecting them from the storm that waited inside for them. As long as they stayed huddled together, watching the sunset from the beach, they'd be okay. It was the words that would be spoken inside that would bring them down . . . she was sure of it. That was why she hadn't moved from where they were standing.

Funny, the wild and roaring ocean was her harbor, and Michael's office was like being out in rough seas.

"Let's go in, babe," he whispered in her ear, pressing himself forward just a touch, making his intentions known.

"It's so beautiful out here. I wish I could just lay in the sand, running my hands through it, allowing my feet to sink deeper until I'm one with the tide. With the water washing over me, I'd be a new woman. Untouched. Not tinged or colored by my past or what I do now," she admitted as the sky turned red and purple.

"You're not tinged, babe. Not then, not now, not ever. I love you. And you don't need the ocean water to cleanse you. Whatever crap you're spewing is just that—BS. You're perfect."

He took her earlobe in his mouth and sucked gently, distracting her so she didn't notice when he led her toward the club.

Wearing rose-colored glasses, Lynx followed him up to his office where he laid her out on the couch. Carefully removing her eggplant-colored swimsuit, he knelt in front of her, worshipping every inch of her brown skin.

He dropped his mouth to her core, swiping his tongue up and down before settling on her clit, where he sucked hard. Lynx's back arched off the sofa as she ground herself into his face. On a breath, "Michael" came floating out of her mouth. When he slipped first one finger and then another inside her, she bucked into his face. When she came, it was spectacular. Different. A beginning and an end all rolled up in one. But only she knew that at this point, so she allowed the ecstasy to rain down over her.

She tried not to compare it to the times she climaxed when she was working. Usually, she desperately tried not to let that happen at all. Most of the time, she faked it, but sometimes it felt too good.

But nothing like what she just felt with him.

With Michael, feelings mixed with the fingers and tongue and cock, making their coupling inherently different. With him, she went off like fireworks over the bay on New Year's Eve.

Every time she came with him, she begged her soul to let this be the beginning of a new life for her. But she always ended up back in her old ways. All she needed to do was quit and let go of her private mission, and Mike would welcome her with all her past baggage. But she couldn't—no matter how hard she climaxed.

Lynx heard him rolling on a condom. Of course, they'd never done it bare. She followed all the appropriate practices and was tested regularly, but rubbers were a must when it came to Michael sinking deep inside her well-used pussy. It wasn't her preferred word, but appropriate in this case. While they didn't fight about much, they fought about this—he hated how many men she let sink deep inside her.

She just didn't get why he continued to dip his very own wrapped-up length inside her. Michael was wealthy and gorgeous. He had strong convictions and the best heart. Why would he waste his time with someone like her?

Like at the moment, he had lifted her as he sat and brought her down on top of him. With her riding him, her legs straddled on either side of his hips, he brought his hand up, brushing the hair out of her face so he could stare deep into her eyes.

"Lynx, babe, this is pure beauty," he said, never letting go of the eye contact, his hand gripping her hair.

She didn't respond, just shut her eyes and rode Michael to his own climax. Then she got off of him and ended it for good.

She had responsibilities that she couldn't ignore.

THE LOUD clack of the knocker on her door signaled the end of her private time with her memories.

Lynx stood and smoothed her dress before walking into the foyer. It was showtime. She was going with her benefactor to a party tonight before she came back to do her duty, and sometime this evening, she needed to get him to authorize her visit with the girls.

ten

"**B**RUNO, OPEN the fuck up," I yelled, banging my fist against the door.

A greasy Cuban, his unkempt black hair hanging over his dark eyes, swung the door open and aimed his Glock .45 between my eyes. "What the fuck you want?"

When I whipped my own piece from behind my back, Chantilly let out a gasp and I pushed her behind me. "The fuck I want isn't you. Get Bruno. Now," I said, pointedly flicking the safety on my gun.

"What is it, Sal?" a voice shouted from down the cavernous hall.

"Bruno!" I yelled. "Get the hell out here and tell me what the fuck is going on."

His loafers made an annoying-as-hell clip-clopping sound as he came down the tile hallway toward me.

I wanted to vomit from all the beige-on-beige decor and ridiculous crystal chandeliers. Who did this asshole think he was? Everything about him screamed white-fucking-trash with new money. Lord knows he didn't make it on the up-and-up.

"Well, if it isn't Big Mike. And my little girl gone wild. Mags called, Chantilly. Told me you went AWOL." His brown toupee slipped a tad as he glanced at his goon. "Put the piece down, Sal."

Pushing his faux hair back into place, Bruno frowned at us. "I need to figure out why my little Chantilly disgraced a big client. By the way, you fucking this one now, Mike? You got a thing for call-girl pussy, my man? Gonna work your way through my entire stable?" Bruno stared me down the whole time, ignoring his *little Chantilly*'s new shiner.

No fucking way he was going to rattle me.

"You bastard," I spat out.

I pointed my gun at the wall and fired, sending ugly beige drywall flying everywhere. Finally, the floor was mine.

"Only one girl for me, Bruno, and tonight I learned you sent her to the wolves. That's right, fucker, your big client happened to mention *Miss Lincoln*. Now you're going to fucking spill."

Taking a step forward, I stood tall, looming my own six-plus feet over his five-foot-eight frame to let him know who was boss.

Me.

Bruno narrowed his eyes on me. "That's none of your business, Mike. My clients are my business, and your titty club is yours."

Shooting out a hand, he grabbed Chantilly by the arm. She winced when he caught one of her fresh bruises, but he ignored her pain.

I stepped up, tapping my piece in my hand. "Let go of her, Bruno. I got a few more bullets in here, and Sal is looking like a great target right now." When Sal brought his Glock up again, aiming his piece and his beady black eyes on me, I said, "Go ahead, Sally-boy, take me out. See if it makes a damn difference with your scum of a boss."

"If you're as smart as they say, Mikey, you'll leave while you're ahead. Now, I need to get a few things straight with my girl here," Bruno said, dragging Chantilly down the hall.

"Stop!" she screamed. It was a blood-curdling, belly-deep scream that nearly made my ears bleed. Clawing at Bruno's hand, she cried out, "You're hurting me."

Chantilly didn't stop at that. No, she kept her foot on the gas, flooring it like she was in a drag race.

"Move back, Bruno! Let me tell you why you're hurting me. I got bruises and scrapes from that prick Rahm getting rough with me after trying to slip me some roofie-shit. I told you this before—I don't do drugs. I have a daughter who needs me!"

Bruno jerked his head back. "Shit, Chantilly. I didn't know they roughed you up."

With that, the idiot shredded the last of my patience. "Where the fuck you been the last five minutes? Who the hell do you think the shiner is from?"

He smirked at me. "You, tough guy. You little cocksucker."

Sweat trickled down my back, and my track jacket felt like a straitjacket. I felt like I was about to come out of my skin, and if I didn't get some answers soon, I was seriously going to start taking people out.

"You're wrong about a few things," I told him. "The shiner for one. That's from your big client. Two, I don't suck cock. And three, I'm not little, but I am tough. Now, do what the lady said and move the fuck back."

Bruno released Chantilly and she returned to me, hooking her arm through mine.

"We're gonna chat, Bruno, and you're gonna tell me all you know about this Rahm and where Miss Lincoln is," I said, inviting myself in and heading toward the sitting room with my gun at the ready.

I'D TOLD Carson we'd talk in the morning, but couldn't wait when I finally got back from Bruno's place. Against my better judgment, I dialed up my buddy at five o'clock in the morning East Coast time, waking him up and dragging him out of bed with his wife.

"So, they roughed up the informant, and then what?" Carson asked after I'd started my story.

I was pacing the length of the pool deck at Asher's Florida house, my feet bare against the chilled stone. The moon was making its way down while the sun was trying to break free, bringing with it a new day.

For me, though, nothing was new. I was still living the same nightmare as the day before.

"He said something about Miss Lincoln not liking a fist up her cunt at first, but now she's happy with her arrangement. A fist up her cunt, Carson. Did you hear that? That's the woman I love they're disgracing." My voice cracked, and I couldn't force any more words through my clogged windpipe. "I hear you, Mike. I do. But you have to calm down and tell me the rest. Then we'll go from there," he said calmly, pragmatic as usual.

I told him about dragging Chantilly over to Bruno's, leaving out everything about the guns and shit. He might have left the FBI years ago, but didn't need to hear about all the illegal actions I'd recently committed—against the mob, no less.

"At first, the ass thought I roughed up Chantilly, but we got that out of the way right quick. Then we got to discussing this Rahm dude. Apparently, he and his buddies roll into town every now and again for a good time. They take up a whole floor of a hotel or some shit, buy enough coke to take out an army, sun themselves by day and fuck by night. They pay triple or quadruple and like their girls all shapes and sizes—gingers, blondies, and darkies, according to Bruno. But the head of their group, he only likes dark. Always wants a Nigerian or Dominican. Do you hear where I'm going with this, man? He likes them dark, whoever the fuck he is."

"Shit." Carson let out a loud breath through the line.

I couldn't stand any more after my rant. Lying down on the gray slate and staring up at the lightening sky, I talked some more.

"This asshole Rahm is apparently the big guy's cousin, an attaché or some fancy crap. He's always the lead on the trip. The head honcho doesn't always show. This time, he wasn't planning on coming. Rahm told Bruno his cousin sent them on a little trip as a present, so they were all in for a good ole fucking time. Bruno told me he said 'no darkies needed because my man is back home with that choice piece of ass you sent him.'" Sighing, I added, "That's what I know."

"Now I know why this was all fucking tied up tight at the agency. Mike, this is no straightforward girl-gone-missing case. It's sex trafficking, and we're gonna have to get a fucking pair of Samurai swords to cut all the red tape in our way. But we're gonna do it," he said, full of false confidence. "I'm gonna get your girl, man. This is the break we needed."

Yeah, you'll get my girl from some fucking sex-trafficking ring and a bunch of rich-as-shit foreigners.

"Fuck!" I yelled into the phone. "I'm cracking, Carson. I gotta get her. Ended shit with Marta. Realized what a fuckup I am to do that. Need Lynx back like I need to eat and breathe."

"We're going to get her," he assured me. "What else did Bruno say? Did he know where they took Lynx? Did he broker the deal?"

A sob raced up my throat, and there I sat crying like a baby on the phone with my friend, the tough-as-nails PI married to a former stripper. Tamping it down, I got myself under control and told him everything else I knew.

"Bruno wouldn't cop to much. Said that he only arranged for their entertainment when they were here, and whatever Lynx set up outside that wasn't his business. As far as he knew, Lynx was living the good life with one of her johns." I could barely push out the last few words, choking up all over again.

Carson sighed. "Listen, I'm not on a case now. I was just hanging with Lila and the baby for a week or so before I start up again. I'm coming down there in the morning."

"No. Fucking. Way," I said, needing to kick that idea in the nuts. "Lila will kill me."

"Yes, I am. And no, she won't. She wants you happy, Mike, like she is. Besides, her brother is here in LA now, and so is Asher's brother, so she has a ton of family to keep her company." Changing gears on the conversation, Carson said, "Look, I gotta roll. I'm calling the hanger to see if I can get a charter. I'll see you soon."

When he disconnected the call, I tossed my phone aside and gripped my head in my hands.

How the hell did Lynx get involved in sex trafficking? And what were they doing to her?

I rolled into the pool, allowing the water to take me under, trying to succumb to the soft lapping and put an end to what I was currently feeling.

Gasping, I came up for air and headed inside for a shower. No matter how much hell I was in, life went on, and I had a meeting with the architect on the hotel.

eleven

H E TOOK her hand, bringing her fingers to his dark lips and kissing softly along her knuckles. "Hello, my lovely Lincoln," he said, running his nose along her wrist, inhaling her scent.

Lynx had been playing the role of an enamored woman for so long, her shudders remained hidden deep below the surface. Her perfectly convincing act carried her a long way, but not quite far enough. She needed tonight like a person stranded in the desert needs a drop of water.

Thankfully, she had never told anyone in this mysterious place her real name. She was Lincoln all the time, and it was for the best. Especially in the beginning when she was at the disposal of so many men, she couldn't bear to hear another man say her birth name. Just the thought of the strange jumble of consonants and one lonely vowel rolling off yet another man's tongue gave her chills.

"Hello, Zayid," she answered dutifully, batting her eyelashes as was expected.

The short man stood in front of her wearing an expensive tan suit, a crisp white shirt, and an ice-blue tie, reeking of cologne and privilege.

He brushed his hand on her cheek. "How are you this evening?"

"I'm lovely," she said—yet another dutiful expectation of her.

"And you certainly look lovely. Is this one of the dresses I purchased for you in London?" he asked, not allowing a minute to pass without his guardianship being noted.

"It is. Thank you." Lynx leaned in and ran her mouth over Zayid's cheek, landing on his leathery lips for a kiss, welcoming him as she was expected to.

He pulled her close, his erection digging into her front as he forced his tongue into her mouth. She willed her tongue to explore his, proving she was worthy of being one of his chosen.

Breaking free, he asked, "Shall we?"

As they left the apartment, escorted by several bodyguards through a series of underground tunnels, Lynx tried to get her breathing under control. She hadn't been to one of the parties since before London. Then again, she'd been whisked on that trip after the last party—when a guest of Zayid's got too close for comfort . . .

LYNX HAD been drinking a cocktail with her long legs comfortably stretched out along a suede chaise, one of the other girls purring by her feet and another lounging by her head. The DJ was spinning some blaring American techno blend that was hurting her ears. There were girls everywhere in a myriad of variations . . . ginger, blond, brunette, freckled, Asian . . . but only one black. That was her—the sole dark woman.

Men perused the room, free to take a sample or a taste of any of the numerous flavors on the buffet spread in front of them. If they liked what they tasted and wanted to savor a bit more, there were rooms along the corridor where they could feast to their content behind closed doors.

Except when it came to Lynx. Her off-limits status was clear by the placement of the lounge she inhabited to the left of Zayid's regal chair.

Of course, while she lay next to his throne, he was across the room running his skinny finger along the brow of an exotic Latin girl who was new to the complex. She sucked on a piece of fruit from her drink, running her tongue all around the limp, pickled piece of nothing, trying to act seductive. It was the same every time there was a new crop of girls. They all wanted to be a favorite, so they labored over ridiculous sensual acts in a desperate attempt to capture Zayid's attention.

It wasn't enough to be paid to suck and fuck whatever rich idiots or heads of state Zayid entertained. No, the girls wanted the promise of trips and gifts and extra stipends. Lynx was the first to admit . . . it was hard not to get greedy when staring such opulence in the eye.

At that last party, she was being a good girl in her red silk gown, showing off for the crowd how lucky Zayid was, when a stout man approached. Both the girl at her feet and the one sitting by her head leaned forward, trying to seduce the portly guy. No one was in the mood for a fight to break out.

But this asshole paid no mind to the other two women and strode directly to the side of the chaise, grabbing Lynx by the hand and pulling her to her feet.

"Why, hello there, you dark piece of meat."

"Please let me go." She spoke quietly, keeping her eyes down while trying to get a glimpse of where Zayid was. He would go ape-shit if this fat fuck didn't move along.

"No way, baby doll. I was told I was allowed to sample the merchandise, and I want to take you back to a room," he said, the stench of alcohol and pot oozing in equal measure from his breath and his pores.

Lynx was trying not to gag when a member of the security detail came up from behind them. The big bald dude with rippling muscles in an all-black suit stepped close and lowered his voice, yet still maintained his menace.

"Remove your hands from the lady."

Smoothing a clammy hand all along her arm, the fat man didn't even glance his way. "Why?"

"Because she's off-limits."

"No fucking way," the fat man scoffed, and the bodyguard grabbed his arm.

"What in hell is going on here?"

Zayid approached from the other side of the room, his accent coming through stronger in his amazement. Lynx wasn't sure if it was because someone had the gall to bother her, or that someone disturbed his other little rendezvous across the room.

The bodyguard tightened his grip on the fat man's arm. "I was just asking this gentleman to move along and remove his hands from Lincoln."

Zayid glared at the man. "I would do what he says. Lincoln is not for anyone but me. That is my seat," he said, pointing toward his large gold encrusted throne, and then gestured to Lynx. "And this is one of my personal women."

Tamping down a wave of disgust at the thought of being someone's property, Lynx stood and smiled like a pageant winner. She almost started waving her hand in the air as if she were sitting on the edge of a convertible in a parade wearing a sash and a crown.

The bodyguard dragged the fat dude out, and later escorted Zayid and Lynx to a private airstrip where they departed to fly to London. In the back of the plane, Zayid blindfolded his prize girl before roughly taking her from behind.

The heavy scrap of fabric caught unwanted tears as Lynx came hard despite not wanting to give in to the sensations crashing through her body. Zayid knew where to flick and pinch, and within a matter of moments, she was squirming and panting. Her braids laid long and heavy on her back while her hands remained trapped—she wanted to rip her hair out by the roots, but her hands were stuck underneath Zayid's heavy torso and her own weight.

"Who is in charge?" he yelled as he pumped himself furiously into her most private spot.

"You, Zayid. You," Lynx answered dutifully.

Slapping her ass, he pumped harder until he pulled out and emptied himself all over her lower back and ass crack, marking her. Smearing her with his dirtiness. Labeling her with shame—if it were possible to wear any more.

She couldn't wait to run and replace his marking with a more permanent one. The tattoo.

TONIGHT, LYNX let out all her fear and apprehension on a long exhale as they approached where the gathering was already in full swing. It was late, close to midnight, but she'd lost all sense of day and night shortly after arriving here. She spent more time awake when it was dark than light.

Almost at the party, Zayid stopped and pushed Lynx up against a wall. The cold stone pressed into her bare back as he said, "Don't be encouraging tonight, Lincoln. Remember who owns you? Me. It was I who took you to London last month, and Hong Kong the month before that. Only I fill your holes. Do you know what I mean, my beauty?"

"Yes, Zayid, I know," Lynx said, lifting her gaze to meet his, something she didn't often dare do, but she needed a favor from him tonight. "It is you, Zayid, who I belong to. Only you."

"Good. Now, let's go have fun. And be ready to go down the hall to my private quarters later. I'm feeling very energetic, my beauty." He

tinged

ended the conversation by running his palm over the side of her breast and sliding his slobbery tongue along her ear.

She waited until they were walking again to allow the cringe to exit her body.

twelve

I WAS A little late getting to the club, so I went straight to the back bar where Carson was waiting. He'd arrived late that afternoon, but I'd been moving Chantilly and her daughter into Asher's house.

The fair-skinned tall drink of water whose real name was Lisa was finally safe. She'd kept offering to pay me rent, and the whole affair took longer than I expected, but was worth it. Now Lisa and her beautiful blue-eyed daughter were set up in a mansion worth more than she'd ever make in a lifetime, and I was late for my meeting with Carson, but I didn't need another missing person on my conscience.

"Hey, man," I said, slapping Carson on the back.

He stood up and pulled me in for a bro hug before returning to his Scotch.

Lifting my chin to the bar back, I said, "I'll have what he's having."

"Like what you did with the space down here." Carson smirked, his gaze wandering the club's lilac decor.

"Shut up. You probably spend as much time in strip clubs as I do. Besides, your wife did all this purple shit."

"How you doing, man," he asked while we waited for my drink, his brown eyes laser focused on me. He was older than me—over a decade—and I took in the hint of gray in his beard, the laugh lines and slight crow's feet. All evidence he was living life, and doing it while smiling.

"Not good, bro," I answered honestly, staring down at my basketball shoes.

Silence hung between us. Carson wasn't Asher. He might be as bossy and protective with his lady and kids, but Carson was different. Schooled in real-world shit, well-educated, and a decorated federal agent, he was calmer, cooler, more pragmatic than Ash. He was the right person to ask for help on this. Asher would have already lost his shit, ridden his bike over to Bruno's, and opened up fire—all before hiring some mercenaries to find the people keeping Lynx.

"You got to have a clear head, Mike," Carson said, interrupting my thoughts. "Getting yourself all tied up in emotion is gonna fuck everything up. Like when I saw Lila's ex drag her into that building, intending to rape her, I had to wait and go in at the right moment. It was hell for me, but my patience got that piece of shit locked up behind bars forever." He ran his hand through his hair and released a long breath. "More important than that, I got Lila back safely."

"I feel you, man, but this shit is fucked up." I tossed back my drink. "Really fucked up. How the hell did Lynx get involved with a sex ring? And why? For fuck's sake, why?" I tamped down the urge to slam my fist on the bar, shoving it deep inside where it formed a knot from all the tension.

"We don't have those answers. If we did, we'd have Lynx. But we're going to get her, you hear me?" He clamped a hand on my shoulder and shook it.

My head bobbing with the movement, I barely heard him over the hip-hop blaring in the background, and the DJ announcing the next girls to take the stage. My mind was a million miles away from the Wave.

"How the hell we gonna do that?" I'd been on my own since I was a teen. I was used to solving shit solo, and I didn't like feeling helpless.

"Leave that to me, tough guy," Carson said matter-of-factly. When I stared at the floor, the deep mahogany hardwood planks eating up my panic, he tilted his chin toward the main stage, changing the subject so I wouldn't have time to wallow in my fear. "You got a sweet thing going on here."

Dragging my head out of my ass, I scanned the club. "Yeah, we're doing well. Way in the black, just like Lila over in LA. Asher may not know much, but the ass knows strip clubs. He's got the formula fucking down."

"Think you do too, buddy. You got more stages down here, and I saw the long line of people behind the red rope, waiting to get in here. Oh, and I also know about the hotel, my man. You know Lila can't keep that shit bottled up," he said, smirking.

I shrugged. "Cat's out of the bag now that Nat knows. We broke ground and the foundation is in. That shit is happening."

Carson's gaze moved back to the stage. "That the one you were sleeping with?" he asked, nodding toward Marta.

"Yeah. I'm stupid, man," I said, running my fingers through my hair. It was growing out. Instead of my usual soft spikes, I was looking more like a shaggy surfer. I'd been so busy moving Chantilly, managing the club, meeting on the hotel, and obsessing over Lynx, I hadn't been in for my regular buzz, another reminder of how even the little things didn't matter anymore.

"Nah, you're just a man." Carson shook his head and eyed me. "But good thing you put an end to it, because that woman is crazy for you. She's giving you a private dance in a room full of ready-to-go spectators."

T HE FIRST thing I felt was fingers running up and down my leg, tracing patterns on my thighs.

"Wake up, sleepyhead," rang softly in my ear as delicate fingers massaged my tired muscles.

God, she's back. Lynx is here. And Carson didn't need to do anything illegal to find her.

"Hey, baby," I said. It came out garbled and groggy.

"Hey," she said back, another throaty whisper in my ear, sliding her taut body along mine.

The air rushed out of me. I could barely breathe from anxiety and excitement.

My cock was erect, reaching for the voice and its owner. I gave it a quick, hard squeeze, silently reminding it to be patient.

Because Lynx is here—in my bed.

A moan escaped from me as she swept her tongue over my ear, trailing a wet, hot path down my neck before swiping that warm, luscious tongue down my chest.

"Come here, baby."

I urged Lynx to kiss my mouth and let me have a taste of what

tinged

I'd been longing for. But she was stubborn and continued her pursuit south, finally landing near my ready-to-explode dick.

"Oh Christ." I let out a long exhale as her warm breath coasted over my tip. Then her whole mouth ghosted over my cock, not really sucking, but lightly tracing its entire length. My mind floated on a bed of clouds. This was bliss.

I leaned my head back into the pillow and blew all the air out of my lungs. My hands reached for her braids, itching to grab a handful, but instead they met soft waves. My fingers twirled through the strands, encouraging her to continue her soft teasing.

I was going to blow as soon as she clamped down.

Then she did, tightening her soft, plump lips around my rigid length, riding me with her mouth. My hips started pumping, pushing deeper into the heat of her mouth. I desperately wanted to come. But I also wanted to get inside her so fucking bad.

I didn't have a choice because she picked up speed while grabbing my ball sac and grazing the tip of my cock with her teeth every time she rode to the top. And I fucking exploded down her throat.

My hips were still pumping when I woke to my hand being a sticky mess.

"Shit," I roared into my empty apartment, before I stood up and stomped to the bathroom to clean myself up from a wet dream.

thirteen

Two weeks later

FLANKED BY two security men on either side, Lynx walked confidently through the courtyard wearing a bright red halter dress and a hot-pink-and-red-striped shawl tossed over her shoulders. The sun reflected off the bald bodyguard's head, and the sound of running water floated from the fountain in the center of the palatial expanse. She couldn't see them but felt the eyes burning into her from above, the ever-present security cameras that protected the compound and watched each and every one of her steps. The sound of her gold-studded sandals echoed off the stone tile as she contemplated making a run for it.

Zayid had been feeling magnanimous two weeks ago and had granted her a few days with the other women at the townhouse—but only while he traveled abroad.

Lord only knows what he's doing in whatever country he gallivanted off to with God only knows who.

Following a long evening in his private quarters, he'd broken the news of the upcoming trip. Lynx had seized the moment with a schooled pout on her face.

"I'll be lonely while you're gone. Can I go stay with the girls? I want to lay by the pool and sun myself for when you get back."

tinged

"Would you like that, my beauty?" He ran a finger down her cheek, letting it trail down her side, making its way to the lacy edge of her panties before finally dipping in and tracing her sensitive spot. "No parties. You'll behave because you're all mine," he said on a growl while shoving his finger inside her.

Lynx had nodded, afraid to open her mouth, fearing what might come out. With his thumb on her clitoris and now two fingers deep inside her, she'd hated herself for being on the precipice of an orgasm. Begging herself not to moan, she'd remained quiet as Zayid skillfully worked her up. He might not be much to look at but he was a dangerously skilled lover, and no matter how many times Lynx scolded herself for feeling anything where he was involved, she couldn't stop the effect he had on her.

But now he was gone and her plan was back in play. What he did while abroad had no bearing on the moment because Lynx got what she'd been driving for—time with the girls.

Nearing the door, she bowed her head in thanks to the security detail before one of them punched in the code for the door and pushed it open, allowing a rush of cold air to smack her in the face. Her hair, loose and curly, caught in the breeze and swirled all around her face, masking her features covered in equal parts fear and excitement.

Dane, the enormous bald bodyguard who had protected Lynx from the fat man, caught her eye. "You're to stay in the townhouse, Lincoln. There'll be someone posted at this door at all times. Zayid's orders. I'll be on the first shift." He moved next to the door and stood at attention at his post.

Although Dane was somewhat new, he'd recently risen to the top of the ranks. Zayid liked him, supposedly because Dane took Lynx's care very seriously. Obviously, he had been tasked with her protection while Zayid was out of the country.

"I know the rules. Thank you," Lynx offered quietly and entered the townhouse without looking back.

She found the other girls lounging by the pool. Feeling at ease, she quickly shimmied out of her dress and scarf and collapsed onto the bright yellow cushions of a lounge chair. Soft music floated from hidden speakers, the scent of coconut oil filled the air, and pitchers of water and sangria lined the side tables.

Lauryn was on her right, completely nude other than black-and-white polka-dot bikini bottoms, and Kimberlie was on her left, wearing a red G-string bikini. They both turned at the same time and said, "Hey, Lincoln. What's up, girl?"

"I'm out, that's what's up." Lynx poured herself a water and sat back in her iridescent purple one-piece suit. It might have been a one piece, but its deep V in the front left little to the imagination.

"You didn't go with the master this time?" Kimberlie turned her attention to Lynx, eyeing her from head to toe.

"No, I'm just happy to be with you ladies. It gets lonely in the apartment. Obviously, Zayid went to the States, so he'll probably be bringing back a new girl or two."

"You're out, but no parties," Lauryn said.

Lynx, unsure if the girl was being matter-of-fact or bitchy, simply nodded.

"Let her be, Lauryn. She's lucky she got out to be with us and isn't MIA like the other black girl," Ginger said, her words dropping to a whisper at the end.

Lynx sat up, slipped her sandals back on, and walked toward Ginger. Sitting on the end of the redhead's lounge chair, she asked quietly, "What happened to her? The other black girl."

"No clue. She was here and then she was gone. Then you arrived. That's it," Lauryn said.

"Hush." Ginger nodded toward the roof where the tiny eyes-in-the sky monitored all their movements.

"Bull-fucking-shit, Ginge," Lauryn said with a scowl. "I'm sick of tiptoeing around Lincoln. She shows up on the scene and in a matter of months, she's the number-one girl and moved into her own place. We should've had a chance when that other bitch went missing." She stalked toward the already crowded lounger. "It's just so fucking convenient that you're half black or whatever the hell you are, because we all know Zayid likes dark meat," she said, leaning over to whisper in her prey's ear.

"Enough." Ginger ran her soft hand up and down Lynx's arm, settling on her shoulder. "We don't know what happened to Sammy. She was here for about a year before she was promoted to the private apartment. She was Zayid's definite favorite, dripping in jewelry and always running off somewhere shopping. Then one day, she was gone."

The freckled redhead sighed before continuing. "I liked her a lot. She was sweet and nice, despite growing up rough, in the ghetto or something like that. Anyway, she was half black like you and caught Zayid's eye almost immediately, although he shared her with us, unlike you. Every once in a while, one of us would get asked to join them in a threesome. Mostly fingering, eating-out kind of stuff. Oh, and using a dildo on Sammy while Zayid watched. He rarely screwed us when she was in the room," she said and threw another quick glance at the cameras.

"She wasn't in my apartment," Lynx said quietly. "Mine is new. Maybe she's still here tucked away?"

Ginger sucked on her straw, the ruby-red sangria coloring its way to her mouth, and shook her head. "No, I don't think so. She was allowed to have a cell phone, and we'd call her from time to time to check in and stuff. She'd tell us about her trips, make plans to come over after she was gone. The line is dead now. Disconnected."

"She wouldn't have just left," Kimberlie said, sliding in beside Lynx on the lounge chair. "Sammy would have made contact somehow, unless something bad happened to her."

Now there were three beauties sitting on one chaise with one great mystery swirling around them.

Lynx frowned. "I'm going to sniff around. I wonder if Zayid has her hidden. Maybe he didn't want to share anymore."

She stood and went back to her own chair. She agreed with the others . . . Sammy wouldn't just disappear unless something was off. But Lynx didn't need to show all her cards right this minute.

ZAYID DIDN'T return for a whole week. It was clear that Lynx was correct and he was in the States, because that's the only place he fell off the wagon to complete debauchery and failed to check in regularly.

After three days with the girls, Lynx didn't want to go back to the lonely apartment, dead set on staying and finishing the job she came for. As promised, Dane had looked out for her at the door for most of the shifts. A few times, she'd run some iced tea down to him, pledging perfect behavior if he let her stay on in the house.

On the morning of the third day, she begged, "Please, Dane. I don't want to go back to the apartment. It's lonely, and I'm having fun here."

He pushed his aviators down his nose and peered over the lenses, raising one eyebrow. "Lincoln, I don't think Zayid'll be too happy with me."

"I'm not going to do anything bad. No parties at night, I swear. Nothing. I just don't want to be alone."

Lynx batted her long fake eyelashes, pleading with the muscular wall in front of her. She wasn't afraid of him. Plus, she was getting somewhere in the Sammy mystery. She needed to stay. With her dark curls fanning all around her face and her mouth painted with sparkly cherry-flavored lip gloss, she gave him her best pout.

"Okay, but the second we get word that Zayid and his detail are in the air on their way back, your ass is hauling back to the apartment. And no parties, Miss L. You hear me?"

"Yep."

With a little pep in her step, she immediately ran back up to the common room where the girls were dancing and singing in their underwear. Of course, many of them were hopped up on something, but not Lynx. She didn't do any of that; she needed a clear head to stay on top of details. Then again, she didn't have to go to a party in a few short hours and sleep with any old cock.

Sitting onto the couch next to Ginger, who was sipping on a glass of sparkling wine, Lynx said, "Hey girl, you good?"

The redhead leaned her head on Lynx's shoulder. "Yeah, just trying to get myself ready for later. You ever think of leaving here?"

"Yep, but I can't," she said, running her hand down Ginger's soft bare thigh.

"I know the money's good, and honestly, what would I do if I left? Go back to dancing in one of those shitty titty bars?" Ginger asked before taking a long sip of her wine.

Lynx got a faraway look in her eyes as they misted over. "Dancing in a titty bar isn't always bad, honey. Back home for me, I knew some great guys who ran a club. The girls made good money and were taken care of, and it wasn't creepy or anything like that," she said, sniffing back tears.

Ginger peered over her wineglass. "Hey, you okay?"

"I'm fine. Just missed home for a minute."

"Do you think you could go back? Would Zayid let you?"

"I'm not going anywhere yet, unless I go where Sammy went," Lynx said with a shudder. "God, where is she? That's so scary."

"Not sure, but I think she either ran or Zayid hurt her. I don't know why I have so many theories, but why do you care?"

Yeah, why did she care?

Because she'd wanted a family her whole life.

Ginger refilled her drink and grabbed a glass for Lynx. The wine's oaky smell filled Lynx's head, mixing with her strange thoughts and delusions of what she would find out in the townhouse.

Apparently, Ginger was through with the serious talk, because she popped a pill and was soon dancing around the room with the others.

fourteen

"Yo, CHAN— I mean, *Lisa*. What's up, girl? All good?" I shouted into my phone.

The club was raging. People were lined up around the corner from the Wave, and inside, it wasn't much better. We'd brought in a headliner for the weekend—a girl from the LA club who went by Aspen. The gorgeous leggy blonde with curves for days and unreal tits had been blowing it out of the water in the City of Angels.

Apparently, word had traveled, and we had a fucking line a mile long.

"Hey, Mike. I can barely hear you, but everything's all good with the house and stuff. I thought you'd want to know the Middle Eastern guys are back, and this time they brought the sheik or whatever the hell he is with them," Lisa yelled into the phone.

NWA blasted from the speaker in the background, but all I could hear was *they brought the sheik with them*. My feet ate up the floor, carrying me toward my office. I threw two fingers up in the air like an airline attendant, pointing toward my private door, and Carson gave me a nod. As luck would have it, he was still in town, considering Lila hand-delivered Aspen to Florida.

"You're not going back there, are you?" I yelled into my phone, making my stance known.

Finally, I was in my office, the music only a faint rumble in the background. Leaning against the steel door, I squeezed my eyes tight.

"No. Bruno's barely been sending me anywhere. He's squeezing me out after the last episode. But Magnolia texted she was going back. She wanted me to know where she was in case anything happened."

"Shit!" I kicked my high-top behind me into the door.

The door opened slightly and Carson yelled, "It's just me."

I moved out of the way, allowing him to enter. I could only imagine what I looked like—wide-eyed and frantic, pacing and swearing and kicking. I was a world away from the prep-school-educated son of a Vegas mogul that I was a few years ago.

"Give me Magnolia's number. I'm calling her."

"I don't think that's a good idea," Lisa whispered.

"Darling, you know I don't give a shit. Give me her digits so I can have my guy talk to her and get a feel for what's going on, babe." Changing tack, I said, "You wanna find Lynx, right? This is our only shot."

"Okay." She disconnected the call and then texted me the contact information.

After I hung up, there was another swift knock at the door. Carson opened it to find Sampson standing outside, a furious look on his face.

"I want in, Mike. She was my friend—not just your girl—and I'm getting in on this," he said, pushing his way inside the door. "I was your first hire down here, if you haven't forgotten, and I've been in on this since day one."

I nodded and told Carson to fill him in while I texted Magnolia. She was en route to the hotel, one other girl in tow, but the Middle-Easterners wanted one or two more. I was reading aloud as the information was texted in, and then I stopped because Sampson was whispering something in Carson's ear.

"What?" I turned on my heel.

Carson spoke first. "You're not gonna like it, but Sampson has a damn good idea. And I think it may be our only shot." He crossed his arms over his chest and leaned against the door, one eyebrow raised, clearly broadcasting that even if I wanted to change his mind, I wouldn't.

Fuck. I was truly fucked.

And that was what I thought before those two idiots shared their plan with me.

fifteen

Landon

SMACKED THE empty tumbler onto the bar and nodded to the
bartender for another. The short guy, not much bigger than my
grandmother and at least as old, hobbled over and poured me a couple
of fingers of cheap Scotch before he scurried off. I ran my hand over
my newly bald head, noting the stubble and making a mental note to
shave it, and tossed back the Scotch.

Savoring the burn, I prayed it would numb me.

I hated this place. It was beyond a hellhole, worse than a shithole. It
was a hell of its very own—hot, dusty, dirty, and full of evil. I despised
the place. Not even the two-bit hookers made it better. Somewhat
ironic to think I could pay next to nothing to get sucked off if I wanted
to. Considering why I was here in the first fucking place, that was a real
shit show.

My phone rattled on the bar, vibrating next to my empty glass, and
I swiped my finger over the ANSWER CALL button.

"Landon here." I tossed a few foreign bills on the bar and walked
toward the door with the burner tucked against my neck.

"What's happening, man?"

"Place is a fucking nightmare. Did I tell you how dirty this shit is

69

up in here?"

"Come on, dude, I know you're staying in some luxury joint. Cut the crap."

I popped my Ray-Bans on, blocking my baby blues from the blinding sun, and made my way down the alley behind the sucky bar.

I laughed for the first time in days. I was staying at some European-branded posh hotel when I wasn't living large in the palace. It was one of the perks of the job, and I'd done plenty of harder time in shittier places over the years.

"I'm in with the guy. So in, you wouldn't fucking believe it. But this guy is bad. Evil as they come, Carson." I kicked the dirt with my boot and watched the dust scatter through the dry air.

"I get that. My friend here has heard only a small part, I'm sure. Sounds like a grade-A cocksucker."

Leaning against the wall, I gave him what he was waiting for. "Got eyes on your girl, and I read your e-mail with your crazy fucking plan. If you want to run roughshod over me, I'm fine with it, as long as it gets me outta here, bro. And of course, I get to take all the accolades."

"Yeah, I know. You can have all the fame and glory. All I got to do is get the new girl out, and my wife and her buddy will be happy campers. No sweat. I'm on my way."

"I got to get back to my cover. Text me on my burner when you get here."

sixteen

L YNX WAS only able to enjoy a few more days in the townhouse before Lauryn found her by the pool.

"Time for you to go, precious one. The king is on his way back, and he needs his queen all cleaned up. Your little crush, Dane, is waiting for you by the door. He sent Ginger to pack your shit." With an evil smirk on her face and an even more evil glint in her eye, she added, "Apparently, there's a big party tomorrow. A few new girls are coming in and some Japanese assholes are coming to visit, so I guess we'll be seeing you again—up on your throne."

Tears clogged Lynx's throat and clouded her vision, but she kept them at bay. Squeezing her index finger into her palm, she felt a tiny flap of skin dislodge. She kept digging, needing to feel more pain. With her finger diving harder, deeper into her own flesh, she pasted on a smile.

"See you then, Lauryn. Thanks for letting me stay."

Dane was at the door with Lynx's bag in hand by the time she reached the bottom of the stairs. She made her way across the courtyard with the sun at her back, but knew there were only dark skies ahead.

Alone again in her condo, the quiet chilled her to the bone. She padded across the floor barefoot, running the pad of her thumb over her newly cut flesh.

Sari came and went.

Lynx drank wine and ate the dinner delivered to her door before passing out.

Sometime around one o'clock in the morning, she heard cars arrive, their headlights beaming on the street below her apartment. Curious, she got up and sat by the window, wondering how many new girls were arriving, and if she would know any of them.

Her heart beat faster at the prospect of seeing a friend, but then wilted at the thought of anyone she knew seeing what she'd become.

LYNX SPENT most of the next day killing time and doing her pre-party routine.

When Zayid arrived early at nine thirty, he reached out and tore her red silk dress right down the middle, the small scraps of outrageously expensive fabric falling to the carpet. Shocked, she tried not to tremble as he ran his hand up and down her back, his finger trailing her spine before his entire palm settled on her ass. The sound of the smack reverberated throughout the apartment, still lingering when another blow came down equally as hard.

"What? I don't do enough for you? You want more? You want company? You disobey me and go live in the common house?" he spat out on the third and fourth slaps.

Pain shot through her skin and settled in her belly before her own pussy betrayed her and started to leak, soaking her tiny scrap of a thong. It had been so long since she'd felt any real emotion, Zayid's anger was more than turning her on.

"What do you have to say?" he screamed, his voice louder than his palm making contact with her ass again and again.

"I was lonely," Lynx said quickly. "Missed you, Zayid."

The bruising slaps ceased, and she was turned around and shoved against the wall. Zayid yanked on a condom and pushed deep inside her, pumping his cock in and out of her traitorous pussy, which was more than ready. Her shoulder bones dug into the old plaster and her legs could barely hold her upright, but she knew better than to disobey at this moment.

When he was done, Zayid said, "Get showered and dressed. We're going to the party, but you're not allowed to talk to any men." His accent was more pronounced than usual. His pulse thumped in his neck, his arteries looking like they were going to pop out of his skin.

Good. Maybe he'll have a heart attack.

But there was no such luck. Lynx did as she was told and got ready for the party, smoothing her wild hair into a long braid and slipping on a yellow satin sheath dress. When she came out to greet Zayid for the second time, he wasn't in the foyer.

"Zayid?" she called, but heard nothing in response. She walked toward the small kitchen and was surprised to find the door to the pantry was open. "Zayid?" she called again, but there was no response.

Looking inside the closet, she found the shelf was shifted slightly to the side. Curious, she peered around it, only to see a closed door. She ran her hand along the wood, trying to open it, but it was locked.

"Holy shit," she whispered. "All this time." Not wanting to be discovered, she hurried back to her bedroom, determined to check it out tomorrow.

A few moments later, she heard him coming from the hallway.

"Are you ready, Lincoln?"

"Yes."

"You look ravishing," he said when he stepped back into her room, caressing her cheek. He could be so charming when he wanted to be.

After escorting Lynx underground to the hidden lounge, Zayid deposited her in her chair. A server brought her a glass of champagne while she surveyed the room.

Content to be alone with her thoughts, Lynx sipped her drink, the colors and textures of the room making her eyes hazy . . . until they landed on the woman in front of Zayid. With her small, curvy frame, her jet-black hair with red highlights straightened down her back, and her boobs shoved into a hot-pink halter dress, she looked oddly familiar.

Squinting to get a better look, Lynx silently wished the other woman would turn around so she could see more than her profile.

seventeen

"I HATE THIS shit," I said into the phone, stretched out on my couch with a bottle of Jack in hand.

"Dude, you have to calm down. I'm here. I've made contact with my guy. He's cool, and working our cover," Carson said. "And ditch the booze. You sound like shit, slurring your words. Dry out and put some clothes on."

"How the hell do you know I'm not wearing clothes?" I stared down at my bare chest and the boxer briefs hanging low on my waist.

"Because I know you. Do you want me to call Asher?"

"No! Don't call him. He'll just ream me out for what we did. You know how he is with his girls."

I stood and headed to my bathroom to flip on the shower, letting steam fill the room while finishing my call.

"Then get your sorry ass to work, and leave this to me."

"Okay."

I hung up and showered—too stressed to even jack it—and went to work.

Wearing my standard jeans, track jacket, and Air Force 1s, I made my way up to the front of the club, wanting to see how the door was running. That was my first mistake.

"Sampson," I told him, "stay away from me. I know you meant well, but you shouldn't have gotten involved. Just keep a distance, and we'll be fine."

One look at my face, and he said, "Yes, boss."

My second mistake was not staying long on the club floor. Like a baby, I went into my office and sulked, memories hemorrhaging in my brain.

It had been one of those rare cold days in Sin City, and Lynx and I had stayed in bed most of the day. I had no clue as to why, but my condo had a gas fireplace in the master suite. I'd turned that baby on . . . and we made love all day.

Lynx was between semesters and had taken the day off to be with me. *All day.* It was before Natalie knew about us, or Asher had mucked everything up for the millionth time. We'd been in our own little cocoon for twenty-four hours.

I ran my hand up and down her smooth back, the tips of her braids nearly touching her ass. I moved them out of the way and let my hand wander over the crack and around the round globes. She was perfect for me. I hadn't told her I loved her, but that didn't mean I didn't want to. The words had been on my lips for weeks. There was something about this jewel of a woman that was made for me.

But her life was fucked up, and I guessed that was why I didn't say it. Was she ready to hear it then? Probably not, but I fucking said it anyway—when I'd been balls deep inside her, gliding in and out slowly, shadows from the flames flickering against the white walls, and all the Sin City bullshit outside my big windows.

My voice had been hoarse and broken when I said, "Love you, Lynx."

Her eyes shot to mine, and small golden embers crackled inside the deep mahogany of her irises. "Michael . . . Big Mike loves me?" She ran her nails down my back and up again while she teased me.

I didn't answer, only kissed her hard, quickening my pace and showing her how I felt. Later, when we were cleaned up and lay with our legs tangled on my bed, she'd said, "I'm starting to care for you way more than I should, but I can't stop it."

That was how we left it for a while until I'd moved to Florida and begged daily, using my love as a convenient reason as to why she should leave her way of life behind.

Now she'd left me behind, and I'd created even more damage in the wake. I cared for another woman, but couldn't give her my heart. I'd hurt Marta, set her free, and then brought her into this like an awful fucking pig.

Carson had put his life on hold for me, left his wife alone with their family to help me. Sampson had meant well, and now Marta had gone to the other side of the earth for me and put herself in harm's way.

And me? In my ultimate moment of feeling low, I called Asher.

"*You what?*" My closest friend screamed at me, and I pictured his eyes bulging out of his head and his hands shoved deep into the pockets of his leather pants.

"She insisted on it. Carson agreed." I banged my head into my desk and ran my hand over the back of my neck.

"Jesus fuck, Mike. I thought you were calling to let me know about our fucking hotel. Now you tell me you sent one of our girls . . . the one you were fucking not long ago . . . to the Middle fucking East to find the last girl you were banging and supposedly in love with? That's what you called to fucking say? Fuck, fuck, fuck you."

I lost count of how many times he said *fuck*, but even I knew it was too many for Asher.

"I know I'm fucked, no matter what."

"I'm hanging the fuck up now and coming to you. When I get there, we're going to figure out how the fuck to get our girls back. I'm gonna have to tell Petey what you did, because he's gonna have to haul his ass here and watch Vegas for me. I got so much fucking cash coming in . . . big conference week here . . . I can't trust anybody but family with this kind of ching."

I leaned back and in my chair and breathed deeply. "He knows. I'm pretty sure Lila filled him in."

I heard Asher kick something through the phone.

"This is my empire, you little shit. Who the fuck gave you permission to take over? Send my girls off on dangerous missions? I guess Lila is the new boss-woman?"

I contained my laughter. He knew damn well she was the boss.

"We wanted to leave you out of it," I explained, but that was only half the truth. We knew he'd be pissed, so we didn't tell him.

"Natalie! Get in here and listen to what Mikey's doing now, all because of your girl. Yeah, I know, babe, I know she took care of Quinn, but this is so fucked up."

Shit.

"I gotta go, Mike. See you as soon as I get there. Better be ready."

He disconnected the call before I could even respond.

Before I could breathe again.

eighteen

A s she sat sipping her wine on the chaise, her long legs extended and the top swells of her breasts on display, Lynx's mind wandered.

Why did this new woman look familiar? And where did the secret passage in her apartment lead?

Every so often, she'd look up at Zayid and smile as if the sun wouldn't rise tomorrow without him, but her head wasn't in the game. So much so, she barely registered him standing to leave. He didn't offer Lynx his hand, but instead made his way toward the new girl.

Lynx pretended not to stare and tried not to squint, but damn if she couldn't figure out how she knew her. She was more consumed with how familiar she felt than the fact her man was leaving without her.

Catching herself, she schooled her expression. If Zayid read any of her actions as being anywhere along the continuum of jealousy to outright disrespectful, she'd pay. Even if he wasn't paying her any mind.

Lynx remained impassive as she watched him take the new girl's hand and bring it to his leathery lips, placing a kiss on her dark skin. She could almost see his body twitching with excitement.

As they left the party room, no one cared. The liquor continued to flow, the music beat almost as heavy as the sexual tension working its way among the visiting men. They took in their fill of looking and caressing any woman they wanted, anyone except for Lynx, who still sat quietly next to Zayid's empty chair.

Security opened and closed the door for Zayid and his new favorite flavor before resuming their positions in the corners of the room. With nothing else to do, Lynx continued to drink her wine, licking her lips and sighing privately. Looked like she was done for the night.

After only a few beats of relaxation, the door opened again and Dane appeared from the hallway. Wearing his usual frown, he walked directly toward Lynx.

"I'm going to take you home now, Lincoln. Leave your drink," he said as he bent down near her ear. He stood and offered his hand to help her up.

She gracefully placed her palm in his and stood, smoothing her dress with her free hand before swishing her hair behind her neck. She'd been leaving her hair down and free lately, but all of a sudden wanted to busy her hands making braids.

"Does Zayid know you're taking me?"

"You're really gonna ask that?" His voice was gruff and curt, making the short hairs on her arms stand on end.

"I was only asking. I usually leave with him after the party, and he's not in the mood to be upset."

"New flavor, babe."

She only nodded and kept her gaze in front of her, but she couldn't help the tiny smile lifting her lips.

Outside, Dane opened the door to a darkened Range Rover.

"No tunnels?"

"Nope. Driving you tonight. Per Zayid's orders, so get in."

She did as he asked and slid into the backseat of the SUV, her dress riding up, exposing her thigh in the moonlight. The leather was soft against the back of her bare legs. When Dane turned the key to the engine, cool air drifted from the vents.

She rested her head against the window and watched the palace grounds shrink in the distance. Tears of relief pooled in the corners of her eyes. She wouldn't be a victim to Zayid's needs this evening. It was a reprieve she'd never imagined being so happy about, but he'd become a little too rough lately, a bit too mean, almost menacing. She'd thought there was no way out of her own mistakes, but the dark beauty with the light eyes gave her a gift . . . a moment's peace from his evil hands and breath.

Oh no, here she was rejoicing. She didn't have to put up with Zayid when this stranger—who looked so familiar—was now stuck attending to his every whim. She shouldn't be so happy, yet she couldn't help but feel grateful.

Lost in her thoughts, Lynx didn't realize they had driven well past her residence.

The car jerked and swerved into traffic, forcing her to look up and see they were now close to the city center. A prickle of apprehension crept up her spine.

"Where are we going?" She wasn't a pushover or afraid to ask Dane. After all, he had proven he could be won with a flash of her smile and a quick peek at her tits.

"Home," he said, not turning around or even glancing her way in the rearview mirror.

She stared at the back of his bald head, the blinking lights of the city reflecting off his smooth skin. Lynx was no fool. She wasn't falling into a trap or saying something she'd regret.

"I live near Zayid in the apartment. He won't be happy if I'm not in the apartment." Beads of sweat formed at the base of her neck, and she could feel her hair curling.

"Home, home, Lynx." This time, Dane flashed her a quick glance in the rearview when he used her real name, and turned the vehicle into the valet circle at a luxury hotel.

"Excuse me? Who do you think you are?"

She wasn't getting out of this car. She might despise Zayid, but she'd asked for this life. As her mom used to say, "I made my bed, Lynx, and someday, so shall you." Lynx had made her bed, and for the most part, it was a comfortable one . . . and she needed to find Sammy for more reasons than anyone knew.

"I'm taking you home. Your friends miss you," Dane said, interrupting her wandering thoughts.

She shook her head. "I live here."

Dane leaned over the headrest and lasered his eyes on her. "I know it's confusing. A touch of Stockholm or something, but we can't sit here and chat forever. I'm getting you the fuck out of here, putting my job on the line, and now I gotta get the decoy out of there too."

"What?"

"You need to go up to room 349. Act like you're staying here." He shoved a fur shawl back toward her. "Wrap yourself in this and go. A guy named Carson is waiting for you."

"No! I can't go back with Carson. He'll tell . . . Michael. No!"

"Who the fuck do you think sent Carson traipsing around the world?"

Lynx continued to shake her head, murmuring, "No. No. I can't go."

"Darlin', I haven't been sweating in this dusty hellhole for the fun of it. I'm getting you out of here. No offense, but this shit is kind of illegal, whatever you're doing over here, your pimp back home introducing you ladies. I'm gonna handle the whole thing after I get you back on American soil . . . which, if I don't do it soon, we're fucked. When Zayid realizes you're not in the apartment, he'll freak the fuck out." His eyes begged her to understand, small crinkles forming in the corners.

"Sammy," she said under her breath.

"What did you just say?" He locked in on her face and stared her down. When she only shook her head again, he demanded, "Speak up, Lynx."

"Sammy. I need to find her."

"What the fuck? Why?" He cocked his head to the side and waited for an answer.

"She's my sister. Half sister. My dad had her a long time ago, about the same time as me, with his other woman."

Dane blew out a long breath. "This is an interesting twist. Fuck!" He banged his head into the headrest. "How didn't anyone figure this shit out?" he muttered, then mumbled a few other swear words to himself.

"She wrote to me in Miami and then showed up at my door one day, telling me about a sheik who wanted her to come live with him. He wanted her to be his sexual servant, harem girl, whatever, in exchange for lots of money and a life of luxury. She was afraid because he'd *met* her through some pimp in Arizona . . . I guess selling ourselves is in our blood, same profession and all that. Anyway, she wanted to know if I thought this shit was legit. I don't know why she trusted me."

Lynx took a long breath. "Then poof, she disappeared. When Bruno mentioned he had this connection, I jumped on it. Jesus, why am I telling you all this like you're some white knight? For all I know, you're playing me too."

She sealed her mouth tight and refused to say any more. This guy made one mention of Carson, and she started running off at the mouth.

"You have to go now, Lynx, and I'll tell you this. I have Sammy or

Samara, so you're in luck."

"What?"

"Go! I'll have to fill you in later. I need to go back and get your lover's friend so I can live to tell you. Go to Carson. Tell him Landon sent you."

THAT NIGHT, they left the Middle East on an unrecorded flight to Grand Cayman Island, where they planned to get on another plane to Florida. The two women sat across from each other bundled in blankets, staring into space.

Quiet reigned the entire flight. No one asked any questions of the women or demanded any answers. Carson messaged people from his phone upon landing in the islands. Dane—who revealed his real name was Landon—typed on his phone too.

All this time, Lynx and Marta remained perfectly mute.

Lynx wanted to see her sister, but she didn't want to see Mike. She also wondered what the hell Marta was doing involved in this . . . and why did she stick her neck out for her? People didn't do that for Lynx.

Or did they?

God, it was complicated. Here she was on a flight back to the States with Carson Graham—the former FBI agent who was married to Natalie's husband's best friend, the former stripper Sienna Flower—to supposedly be greeted by her very own ex-lover, the man who held her heart.

Big Mike Wind.

Michael.

Part Two

Part Two

nineteen

Six months later

LYNX CLOSED her eyes as she bent over into downward dog. Breathing in through her nose and then exhaling, she tuned out everything but the instructor leading the class, calling out poses, encouraging them to breathe and clear their minds. For seventy-five minutes, her mind enjoyed a respite from the nonstop chatter and self-berating that was all her own doing. Through the entire series of balancing poses, Lynx freed herself from thinking about Michael and how she'd mucked up both his life and hers.

Mostly his.

In the final pose, she lay like a corpse and enjoyed her last few moments of solitude. As soon as the instructor released them, reality smacked her square in the chest.

Literally. As she stood to fold up her mat, someone bumped into her.

"Excuse me," a peppy, light, and airy feminine voice said in her ear.

Lynx turned toward the woman who had run into her.

Marta. *The other woman.*

But she really wasn't the other woman because Lynx had left, vanished. It was Lynx who had decided to up and run to a dangerous foreign land under self-deprecating pretenses, looking for her own bounty—her sister. In doing so, she'd ruined her life, as well as Dane's—or Landon's, or whoever the hell he was. And she'd destroyed Mike and Marta's chances too.

Marta could have made Mike happy. They could have had a life. Probably a good one.

Of course, Marta had fallen hard for Mike. Who wouldn't? Except he'd been stuck on her—Lynx.

"No worries," Lynx muttered and continued to gather up her yoga props.

"Oh. Hey, Lynx. I didn't know you went here," Marta said in a friendly tone. Of course, the one woman who was forced to have her heart broken because of Lynx was the nicest person ever.

"Yeah, I got a membership a few weeks ago." Lynx frowned, already reconsidering the one-year membership Asher had given her.

"Nice. I hear you're back in school."

Fucking Mike. Could he just forget her or something?

Trying not to roll her eyes, Lynx said, "Taking a few summer classes and seeing how I like it."

Marta smiled at her. "Asher's here for a few days. He told me you went back to school. I thought that was awesome. I should do that too."

Lynx was wrong. It hadn't been Mike who'd told Marta, but Asher. Maybe Mike had moved on?

When she'd come back, Asher had been in Miami, pacing like a lunatic, waiting for her and Marta to arrive safely. Lynx had never been super close with him, but since he'd married Natalie—the one person Lynx really adored—she couldn't help but gravitate to the generous yet gruff man.

He'd held her while she cried.

He'd rented her an apartment . . . big enough for her sister too.

He'd given her computer work she could do at home, and set her up with tuition for school.

He'd gone home and sent Natalie to stay for a few days. Nat had set Lynx up with a therapist, who she quit immediately.

Asher was determined to get Lynx's life back on track, even when she wasn't so sure if that could be done.

"Oh, that's nice. I mean, that Asher's here, but if you want to go back to school, that's nice too. I guess Asher's keeping up with the hotel project?" Lynx stumbled over her words, unsure if she should be standing here talking to this woman.

tinged

Lynx didn't have to feign interest in Asher. After all that he had done for her, she was invested in the strip-club owner with a heart of gold. Or platinum.

But Marta?

"Yeah. It's going pretty well. Ahead of schedule. Anyway, he said you're thinking of going back to school for a degree in business. Sweet!"

Christ on a cracker, this Marta is too nice for her own good.

What was it to her? Why did she care?

Lynx nodded. "Yeah, maybe. I'll see what happens. How about you? How are you doing?" She could at least try to be nice—this chick had put her life on the line for her.

Marta reached out and ran her palm down the length of Lynx's arm and back up again, leaving it on her shoulder. With their skin together, they could pass for sisters. It made sense why Mike gravitated toward her, but their personalities were polar opposites. For every ounce of Marta's optimism, Lynx oozed buckets of pessimism.

"I'm good, really. I was only in that sick place for a minute, but you? You lived there a long time. A year, right? Sometimes, late at night, I worry about you."

Really?

Lynx stepped back, granting herself some much-needed personal space and freeing her arm as she went on the defensive. She'd made a choice and now she was moving on—or so she convinced herself. There was no reason for her to keep reliving her choices, yet she did.

"It was my choice. My doing."

Marta cocked her slight hip to the side, the bone protruding through her hot pink yoga pants, her messy bun flopping to the opposite side. "You should come down to the club, have a cocktail or something."

"I'm really trying to get my shit together, but thanks for the offer."

"Shit, I didn't mean it like that. It's just I had to go back to work . . . I didn't mean you."

Lynx frowned. The conversation was getting increasingly more disjointed.

"It's cool, Marta. Let it go, okay? I gotta go. See you around."

Lynx tossed her yoga block and water bottle into her bag and headed toward the door.

"He's not doing so well, you know," Marta called after her. "Puts on a good face and all that, but he's a wreck. If you could just let him see you, see you're doing okay . . . please, Lynx? Let him cast his eyes on you."

Why, oh why, does she have to be so nice?

Lynx didn't answer or even bother turning around. If there was one person she didn't want to see, it was Mike.

She was dirty, tainted goods, not deserving of all the beauty that man brought with him.

Why couldn't he watch Marta dance and fall for her all over again?

S AMARA WAS on the love seat when Lynx arrived home from yoga, her legs tossed over the armrest, her hands moving briskly across her drawing pad.

She was making slow progress in healing like Lynx, but better.

Apparently, life on the other side of the fence hadn't been as great as Lynx had always believed. While Lynx nursed daddy issues her whole life, Samara had dealt with self-esteem blows. One after the other, their dad had thrown emotional punches.

Samara has evil eyes. She needs more curves. She'll never make a man happy. She's a stupid white girl in a black woman's body.

Lynx learned of all this after the two had been rescued. Landon had dropped Samara off with Lynx after picking her up from spending time with a friend of his.

Apparently, Samara had been pretty hopped up on pills toward the end of her stay with Zayid, a fringe benefit of blowing your security detail on the side, so she'd spent some time drying out once they made it back to the States. Going above and beyond, Landon had set her up with a friend of his—a woman named Mariah—who helped get Samara somewhat straight.

Mariah had comforted Samara, but she craved family, something she'd never had. Shacking up with Lynx had been a dream come true for her.

It was mutual. It was all Lynx had ever dreamed of too . . .

T HE NIGHT she'd arrived, Samara had come clean, explaining how their dad had been just another prick in a long lineup of pricks they'd come to know. She told Lynx about all the awful things he used to say.

"I wish I would've looked for you sooner. When my mom told me, I was mad for so long," Lynx had muttered into Samara's shoulder as the two embraced on the couch.

Too many tears were shed that evening, but it had to be done.

"I'm sorry," Lynx told her sister. "I was jealous. You had our dad and I didn't. My mom told me your name, Samara Bennett, and I couldn't help but dream about the man with the last name Bennett."

"You didn't know," Samara whispered back, sliding Lynx's braids out of her face.

"But I could've been there sooner. I could've told Mike or Carson or someone. I didn't."

"How did you finally find out where I was? I thought I was completely under the radar."

Lynx stared at the floor, embarrassed to admit the truth. "I knew a guy, a client, who was a DEA agent. One night after we were finished, I mentioned finding you to him. The next time I saw him, he gave me the name of your old pimp. From what I gathered, he sold some info to the Feds, and in his statement, he mentioned getting a pretty penny for an introduction to you."

Samara shook her head. "I can't believe it. Stew was always a creep."

"Lucky for you that Stew told someone. That must be where Landon got his tip from."

"I'll have to ask him one day. We haven't really talked about it."

"You only have to talk about what you want."

"I know. So, after the agent told you, what did you do?"

"I started sniffing around about getting over there . . . with the sheik. Mike was antsy for me to get out of the trade, but I was in too deep. It wasn't fair to him, but I couldn't leave my inner circle. Then it was blind luck when Bruno mentioned his contact."

"Thank you, Lynx. Thank you for risking everything for me. Thank you a million times."

The pair had ended back up in an embrace, crying it all out, hugging each other and never wanting to let go.

"Now I have a sister," Lynx had whispered.

"Me too," Samara had whispered back.

"HOW WAS class?" Samara asked now, stretched out with a cranberry-colored chenille blanket tossed over her legs, and the news on.

Watching the news had become somewhat of an obsession for her. She was paranoid someone was coming to get her or war was starting . . . or any number of crazy scenarios. Her therapist told her to stop, and advised Lynx to ignore her conspiracy theories when she picked up Samara one day. At least Samara still went to the shrink, unlike her. Apparently, once Sammy felt safe again, the doctor had said, her fears would begin to dissipate.

"Eh, Marta goes to that gym. I should've known when Ash gave us the membership . . . probably all the girls at the club belong there. But since I've been going early in the morning, I've missed them."

Lynx sat opposite Samara in a taupe chair, her legs tucked under her, and pulled her hair out from the bun. With her braids falling down her back, she blew out a breath. "She all but begged me to see Mike. Said he's doing bad."

Samara clicked off the TV. "Yeah, Landon said he heard the same from Carson."

"What? How often do you talk with Landon?"

"He calls me sometimes. To catch up."

Lynx thought that was definitely interesting, but didn't push. He'd certainly looked a lot different the last time she saw him. His black hair had grown out into a short buzz, and he'd not been wearing his frown. In fact, he'd even smiled a little, his teeth white and straight.

"I'm going to shower, and then do you want to take a walk on the beach?"

"Yep. I'm off today, but tomorrow, I have a double. Sunday, gotta love drunk men and their football."

Samara was bartending at a chic steak place, making serious bank on tips. Over the last few months, she'd developed a following who came in during her shift.

"Give me ten."

Lynx hit the shower, hurrying because for the first time in a long time, she allowed herself to think about seeing Michael.

Visions from the night she got off the plane bombarded her. In her mind's eye, she saw him standing there, his jeans stretched on his wide thighs, his track jacket zipped up tight, and basketball shoes only partly laced on his feet as he waited for her.

She'd ignored him, brushing by him and heading into Asher's open arms—a man she barely knew in comparison.

twenty

THE CLUB was packed. It was New Designer Fashion Week or some shit in Miami, and we were definitely feeling the surge . . . in a good fucking way.

Sampson held the back door open for me; he'd driven me over to the hotel and waited while I checked on the day's progress. Place was almost done. Once we'd leveled the lot, shit went up quick with Asher paying top dollar.

"I'm going to check on the front, and then see what Staci needs, okay, boss?"

I nodded, and Sampson split off down the hallway while I went to my office. I wasn't needed on the floor at all. Staci had the place running tight. Last month, Playboy called to interview her. She was officially the youngest woman to run a gentleman's club. It didn't hurt she had Asher and Lila backing her, but still . . . I couldn't help but be proud.

Speaking of pride, my dad was right proud of me. In a few months, I was going to follow in his footsteps and be a hotelier.

With no one or nobody waiting for me at home.

Congratulations, Michael Anthony Wind! Not even a college

graduate and a rich motherfucker, a soon-to-be hotel proprietor and heir to the Wind hotel fortune. Hell, heir to your mother's family money too. You're one fucking amazing guy.

Asher had told me to be patient and happiness would come to me. What the hell did he know about doing that? He'd blasted into Natalie's life and never left after he found out her kid was his. He was no Oprah.

Seated behind my desk at the Wave, I checked the monitors. Every couch and seat was full. I caught Sampson chasing Staci around the floor until his palm met her lower back.

"Fuck," I grumbled to myself. Those two were involved . . . I fucking knew it. I'd thought it for some time.

Oh well, she needed a big man at her side. At six five and three hundred pounds of muscle, Sampson wasn't going to let anyone get in her way. So, there you have it. The strip club owner marries the bouncer, or some shit like that.

Hey, I was a bouncer for the last decade or more. Yeah, now I owned the joint and was building a hotel, but I'd always be a protector at heart. I'd wormed my way in with Asher years ago, showed up on the Tunnel's doorstep, and now fucking look at me.

Only thing missing was my lady, who wouldn't only not look at me, she wouldn't give me the time of day.

I got that she'd been through hell, slept with a bunch of johns and had been Girl Number One to some freaking rich-ass sheik. I still wanted her, no matter how broken she was. I'd put her back together, stitch her up inside and out, and love her until she was whole.

Didn't she get that?

Yep, it was that time of day when the melancholy took over . . . another thing Asher warned me about. He'd fished me out of the bottom of a bottle many a time; now he didn't want me deep diving into Jack anymore.

I pulled a bottle out of my drawer and grabbed the shot glass from the corner of my desk. I tossed back two shots of my main man and leaned back in my chair. I'd let my hair grow long again, so I shoved it out of my eyes and squeezed them tight.

Behind my eyelids, there she was . . . Lynx. Pretty, serene, her braids let down, her eyes sparkling. She was smiling at me.

I lost myself in the vision . . . and then my office door banged open.

"Please stop sending people to check on me." Lynx tripped through the doorway, not tipsy but full-on loaded. Her ass hit the floor and she curled up into a ball, the flimsy white tank she wore hugging her figure.

tinged

"Please," she repeated from the fetal position, her dark nipples poking through the tank.

Shit, she wasn't wearing a bra. *Did she just walk through the club like that?*

My mind warred with my body. I wanted to stomp out to the club floor and smack anyone who'd looked at her like that.

Sampson poked his head around the door. "Sorry, boss, but she shoved her way to the front of the line and demanded to see you. Luckily, I was there. Brought her through the back, but she slipped away from me."

"It's fine." I stood from my chair and walked toward the broken woman on the floor, now half-crying, half-laughing. I picked Lynx up and ran my hand down her back. "Shhh, babe."

She squirmed for a beat or two and then settled her head on my chest. "It hurts when they talk to me about you," she muttered.

"Go ahead, shut the door," I told Sampson. "I don't want to be bothered."

He nodded and walked out.

"I want you to move on," she murmured. "But there you are, always looming. *Mike's not doing well. He's worried about you. Mike puts on a tough face . . .* don't they know your name is Michael?"

Although slurred, her words warmed me up, coating me in a parka I didn't know I needed.

I sat on the sofa, keeping Lynx in my lap. She smelled like tequila and the beach.

Moving her braids aside, I whispered in her ear. "Babe, you need to calm down. I'm worried about you, but I'm not going to ever stop doing that."

She shook her head against my chest. "You have to stop."

I ran my hand down her back. Tremors shook her as my fingers made their way over her damp tank, goose bumps forming in their tracks. She sucked in a breath at my touch.

"That's like telling my heart to stop beating. I can't not check on you. Knowing you're alive and surviving is oxygen to me."

"Marta's good. Better for you," Lynx mumbled, placing her hand on my arm.

"She's not. I'm not saying she isn't a good woman and that I don't care for her. I do. But she's not you, and she knows that. Always knew that."

"Why is she so nice to me? I'm nothing but garbage."

"You're not garbage. Don't ever say those words again. They hurt me in a way you'll never know. Let's not talk about this. You're wasted, and the alcohol is jumbling your mind."

Her fingers lingered on my forearm, finally shoving up the sleeve of my shirt and tracing my tattoo, her red-painted nail running along the cursive C. It was hypnotic.

"Michael," she whispered before passing out in my arms.

That was pretty much how I spent the night, sitting up on the couch of my office as Lynx slept in my arms. It was the best night I'd had in a long fucking time.

twenty-one

LYNX WOKE up groggy and not at home. Her body ached and her throat was drier than sandpaper. Her palm caught along her leg, slightly fresh cuts of her own doing scratching her smooth skin.

Opening her eyes and looking up, she found Michael staring back at her. Quickly taking in her surroundings, she realized she was at the Wave.

His hand found her back. "Morning."

She closed her eyes again and took a deep breath, unable to make sense of why she was waking up in the Wave, in Mike's arms no less. Had he slept like that all night? Sitting up?

"This can't be good," she murmured.

"It's better than good. You had a bad night, and you came to me. That's what you should do."

She shook her head and tried to squirm out of Mike's grasp, but he held her tight. Not painfully so, just enough to hold her in place.

"Mike," she said, the word coming out rough.

"Michael," he said, correcting her.

"I need to go."

He shook his head. "Let's get you cleaned up, and after we get some breakfast in you, then you can roll."

Lynx tried, but she couldn't help her hand from moving to his cheek, and ran her knuckles over his scruff. "We can't."

His forehead met hers. "We can."

"Why? I'm a mess."

"I don't care. Loved you since we first met and plan to love you forever, messy or not. Since the night on the balcony, Lynx."

"Mike."

"Michael."

"Please . . ."

"Not this time. I let you scam me for years. Working the streets, leaving the country. Now you're back and no more scamming. I want you to do everything you want, be anything you want . . ." *Except sell your body.* "But first I want to feed you."

She leaned her head against his shoulder and sniffed back tears. His hand moved slowly up and down her back, and a chill ran up her spine when her sheer tank lifted, exposing her tattoo. She reached back to yank her top down, but felt Mike's finger cresting the wave on her back.

"This is new," he said softly, his words catching in his throat.

She nodded.

"Is it our waves? The ones we watched while you were tucked tight in my arms?"

Lynx nodded again, but she didn't tell him about the hidden words. The moment was already too emotional.

Mike patted her back and urged her to sit up, then stood and reached out a hand. "Come on. Let's get some food in you."

Seated in Mike's work SUV a few minutes later as they drove away from the club, Lynx asked, "Can I go home and change?" She pressed the button to lower the window, breathing deeply of the salty air that rushed inside the vehicle.

"You'd have to tell me where that is."

"You mean you don't know?" she asked, her voice raspy from the night before.

Mike glanced at her. "I could've, but I didn't ask. I let it be for you."

She nodded. "The Ocean Towers. Asher set it up. Of course."

He nodded and drove in the direction of the exclusive high-rise on the opposite side of the beach from his.

"I'm sorry I barged in last night." Lynx cleared her throat. "I shouldn't turn to you. I don't deserve you, but it's all getting to me—"

"Babe . . ."

"No, don't say anything. I need to admit I messed up. I went on this one-woman mission, ended up selling my body and my soul. Now, I'm a mess. And I'm being kept by Asher's money."

"He's got a big heart. I can't let you say that."

"I know, and Natalie has him by the balls, so he has to. But everyone . . . everyone won't stop talking about you. Even Marta—"

"Marta? She's not bugging you, is she?" He turned toward her, his eyes searching for the truth.

"No. She wants me to be with you, take care of you, accept you accepting me. Which is crazy. I'm nothing but a washed-up whore." A single tear fell and dropped onto her tank.

Mike swerved off to the side of the road, slamming the SUV into park before pushing his hand behind her braids and pulling her face close. "Don't ever fucking say that again. You fucking hear me? You saved your sister."

Lynx shook her head. "No, Landon did."

"It's in the rearview, Lynx. You're out and safe. Samara is out and safe. It's time to look forward."

She couldn't even look at him. With her gaze fixed out the window, he checked his mirror and pulled out into traffic.

twenty-two

I PACED THE sidewalk in front of Lynx's building. Thank fuck she asked me to wait outside. My blood was boiling over, anger and hatred rolling off me in monsoon-sized waves.

Washed-up whore . . .

I slid my finger across my phone and found Carson's contact. Pressing it, I paced impatiently as I waited for him to answer.

"What's up, Big Mikey?"

Of course, he answered like shit was coming up roses. And for him, it was—I couldn't begrudge him that.

"I need another favor."

"Name it."

Setting my pride aside for the millionth time, I said, "I thought if I gave Lynx space, she'd come around. She's not. She's wallowing in self-pity, and it's getting unbearable. I need to do something. Now."

"She's been through a lot. Lila didn't see half the shit Lynx did, and she was messed up for a long time. You can't rush her."

"I can't stand by and watch it anymore. I'm sick of being some innocent bystander, so I'm calling in backup. I need you to find her some PTSD shrink, a good one. Someone that isn't going to let her quit so easily, and then I need Lila and Nat to come and convince her to do it. They need to talk or whatever it is they do, and tell her it's time."

"You can't force her, Mike."

I kicked the shit out of my tire, not giving two fucks I was ruining my shoe. "I am and I will."

He exhaled into the phone. "I'll talk with Landon and see who he recommends. He's got to know a person or two. But you need to call Lila yourself. You've been ignoring her, and she's good and pissed. No way am I asking her for you and getting myself in the doghouse. Ask her about the new baby and butter her up."

I nodded, even though he couldn't see it. I knew she'd be mad—I'd forced my way into her problems years ago. Of course she'd expect to be intimately involved in mine.

Running my hand over my head, I agreed to call Lila and disconnected the call.

I stared at my reflection in the car window. I was a mess—dark circles under my eyes, and fucked-up, unruly hair—but I didn't care. I'd take better care of myself when Lynx was better.

My pulse raced . . . where the hell was she?

Staring up at the building, I decided to give her five more minutes, and then I was busting my way in there.

Apartment 1203. Of course I fucking knew where she lived; I just wasn't stupid enough to tell her. It wasn't a huge deal. Asher had eyes on those two, and I was privy to every freaking move—the gym, Marta wading in when she shouldn't have, and stupid Samara sneaking off to see the goddamn federal agent, Landon. I needed to know like I needed oxygen.

My feet tore up the sidewalk, marching me toward the building's front entrance, when Lynx reappeared wearing a loose white tank and jean cutoffs, her braids framing her face. On her feet were all-white Air Force 1s, the same pair I'd bought for her way back when. It must mean something . . .

"Ready?"

She nodded and climbed into my SUV, refusing my help and using the running board.

"You up for the diner? Or you want something nicer along the beach?"

I'd take her anywhere she wanted to go, but I got the sense she needed to feel in control. I'd let her have that small morsel.

"Diner's good. I'm not really in the mood to see and be seen."

My glare could have killed; I felt my own vicious stare mocking me from the windshield. I was getting sick of Lynx putting herself down, and was no longer willing to allow her to decide.

So much for letting her have some control . . .

"On second thought, let's go to News Café."

"Oh, so you pick the most popular place on South Beach, the place every Tom, Dick, and Harry wants to eat at because Versace ate there before he was shot?"

"Yeah, I like it there. And fuck it, you look worthy of being seen."

No one ever said I was nice.

"How's school?" I asked, changing the subject. My mind was made up, and she knew it.

"I'm liking it. It keeps my mind busy. Thinking about asking Asher for a waitressing job. Marta said I should come to the club, and I thought it was a stupid idea at first, but then thought about how I hate being home . . ."

A growl bubbled in my chest, but I did my best to tamp it down. "It's my club, babe. You can ask me."

"Would you say yes?"

"Nope."

"That's why I'm going to ask Ash. He'll say yes."

I shook my head in disbelief, annoyance rushing through my veins, anger boiling in my blood. "Lynx, you're not waiting tables in my club. You want a job? Get an internship or apply at one of the boutiques. You've spent enough time with your goods on display."

"I thought you ran a reputable place."

"I do, but you're fucking mine. In case you hadn't noticed, I've been holding my heart in a bulletproof case for you since you disappeared. I put up with certain shit before, and now I'm not."

"You didn't really," she said, stumbling over her words.

"Didn't really what? Put up with certain shit? Damn straight I did." My blood pressure was shooting up, pressure pounding in my temples. This whole lazy morning was heading in a direction I didn't like.

"I mean, you didn't exactly hold all of your heart." She flicked her hair behind her, the whooshing mimicking the air rushing out of my lungs.

"No, not exactly," I said in self-disgust. "It wasn't a smart thing, but Marta knew the score and I was lonely. Fuck it, I was an ass, lonely or not."

"I don't really care. No one, including me, knew if I was ever coming back. Now, I'm back and I'm a mess."

"I care," I said in a whisper that came out hoarse. "I knew it was wrong. Felt it deep in my gut, but part of me wanted to save Marta in a way I didn't save you."

"Whatever. Plus, you put up with all that other certain stuff, so I guess we're even," she said, tossing my own words back at me.

My truck veered right into the curb as I yanked it over. "Don't *whatever* me. I hate myself for doing it. Probably will never forgive myself. And if you don't, I get it."

"Well, it's not like I wasn't with Zayid, so it doesn't matter."

"He was a job. A mission to find Sammy. Marta was more . . . I cared for her. Not in the same way I love you, but she was—"

"Is," Lynx said, correcting me.

"*Is* a friend, and she knew where my heart belonged. With you."

I traced her jawline with my thumb, my hand shaking. "I know what you're doing, this push-pull shit. You're not damaged goods, or whatever you've talked yourself into believing."

Her gaze remained cast downward, but I could feel her pulse beating throughout her body.

"You're a beautiful woman, even more beautiful on the inside, life beating vibrantly through you. And you're mine."

I didn't wait for a response. I was sick of waiting.

Wanting.

Begging.

Searching.

Leaning in, I replaced my thumb with my lips, running the length of her jaw and back, up her cheek and over her lips. Closed mouth, my lips melded to hers, and I inhaled deeply, breathing my fill.

Our mouths remained closed but something passed between us—a silent promise to make it right. My hand itched to run the length of her bare arm, and my body longed to pull her over the console and on top of me, but I didn't do either. I kept my hand on her chin and my lips fused to hers. I'd take the crumbs.

"Michael," she whispered, the sound like medicine to my soul.

"Lynx, we're going to fix this, I swear." My breath caressed her cheek. "One day, not long from now, you're going to be married to me, my baby in your belly, eating ice cream in bed and laughing like none of this ever happened, your past only a distant memory and a bright future ahead of you. Swear to fucking God, a god I don't even believe in, babe. It's going to be so good, our life."

A tear slipped from her eye, and I kissed it away. "C'mon, let's go eat. Enough of the sadness."

I was done being gentle. It was time I took charge and pushed us in the right direction. So what if talk of babies and marriage was too much, or if I was coming on too strong—I was Michael Wind, destined for greatness. Fuck it all to hell.

Seated in a booth at News Café—with blue water to the horizon outside, and tourists and locals rushing in and out—I ordered an unsweetened iced tea, egg whites and spinach, and toast. Lynx opted for coffee, grapefruit, and some kind of fruit-covered oatmeal.

She was quiet while we waited for our food, and I let her have that moment, making small talk and people watching.

"Feel better?" I asked after she'd taken a few bites.

"Yeah, I needed some food in my system."

"What's your plan for today? Classwork? Gym?"

"Not much. Probably yoga, hang with Sam, make dinner."

"We should go see Chantilly. She's been worried about you."

"Where is she?"

"At Asher's house, the one I used to stay at. I set her up there with her daughter when Bruno went fucking crazy."

Lynx's brow wrinkled as she muttered, "Bruno."

"You haven't heard from him, have you?"

She shook her head. "Pretty sure he's long gone, or I would have. I wonder what he's up to, or if he's worried about me."

"Good choice for him to be long gone. He wasn't going to make it here, not with Carson and Landon involved now."

"He didn't mean to get me involved."

"Lynx, I mean it. Leave the past in the rearview. I don't want to hear you defend Bruno. I can't. You have to understand what that does to me. He put you in the worst place possible, stole you right out from under me."

Her eyes stayed fixed on her coffee. "It's just I needed to find Samara. I don't know, I was all messed up. She's my only blood."

"Maybe so, but now you're going to live life. Maybe talk to someone?"

She shook her head.

"How's Nat?" I asked, changing the subject again.

"She's good. Busy with Quinn, keeping Asher calm. I miss her and Quinn. They were such a big part of my life. I haven't met the babies, Lillie and Parker, either."

"We should go see them all. Maybe Lila and Carson could meet us in Vegas for a weekend?"

"Maybe. I can't think about it now. It's too much. Jeez, I can't even."

"You tell me when. I'm not going anywhere, you hear me? No rush."

"Yeah."

"Samara could come too. Wouldn't that be fun?"

A small smile spread across Lynx's face. It didn't quite reach her eyes, but close enough. I put that there, and I planned to do it more often.

"I WAS BEGINNING to think you lost my number."

That's how Lila answered the phone when I called. She was the sweet one, so I knew I was in deep trouble. Natalie would have said, "Fuck you, Mike. Don't call me for months, and now you call with a favor?" Not Lila. She just internalized her hurt at my not calling.

"Nah, Lila. Just been a rough few months. I hated unloading on you. You've had enough bad shit hanging over you, and you finally got your sweet, second baby and all. You need to enjoy it. By the way, how's the princess?"

Standing in my barren apartment, I leaned my back against the glass, the Atlantic lapping away behind me. I'd begrudgingly dropped Lynx at her place after breakfast, watching until she disappeared inside the front doors of her building, and hoping she'd agree to see me again soon.

"Mikey, I can enjoy my life and still be there for you. Would I even be where I am today without you? Don't answer that, because the answer is no. And the princess, Francesca, is a screamer. Yikes, Carson may be smitten with her, but she's got some lungs."

My head against the cool glass, I blew out a long breath and smiled. I couldn't help but be happy for Lila and Carson. Two kids, a big home, and a happy life.

"Personally, I'm barely holding it together. Staci and Sampson are keeping shit together at the club. The hotel's happening, but Lynx isn't. She's stuck in a bad place, Lila. I need her out of it, done with that crap."

"She's a woman." Lila's voice was gentle, soothing my anger. She'd been a rock, escaping a violent husband and religious oppression, reinventing herself as a stripper and escaping a violent kidnapping.

"You got out of it, made peace time and again. I was there, watched you. Remember?"

"We're all different. We handle stress differently. I'd met Carson, and he showed me I could."

"So I'm not enough?" I paced the hardwood floor wearing nothing but jogging pants hanging low on my waist, naked from the waist up—the way Lynx always loved me.

"You're more than enough, but you need to show her, not tell her. Showing doesn't mean sending flowers and singing telegrams. It means being patient and steady, by her side."

"I think that's what I did today . . . I don't fucking know. I just want her back, all of her, one hundred percent this time. In my house, in my bed, all mine."

Lila laughed into the phone. "Don't get so alpha, Mike. Is she seeing someone again? Talking this out? Ash said she ditched the last person."

"That's why I called. She's not, and I need her to. Carson's getting me a name, and I was kind of hoping you and Nat would help me convince her."

"You're a sneaky sucker. Weaseling your way into my love life back then, and now this. But I'll help. What do you need?"

That was the problem.

I had no fucking clue.

twenty-three

Two days had passed, and I was sitting in my office with my feet thrown up on the desk, wondering how long I needed to wait to call Lynx when there was a knock on my door.

"Come in." I was sure it was either Staci or Jovi. They'd been out front setting up for the night.

When the door didn't budge, I finally stood the hell up and pulled it open, completely unprepared for the sight in front of me.

"Hey," Lynx said, standing there in a sheer white T-shirt, jeans, red Chucks, and her hair down and smooth.

Swallowing equal parts lust and surprise, I moved my gaze up from the red triangle bikini top showing through her shirt, and met her eyes. "Hey. You okay?"

We stood there like two strangers, unsure which way to move to let the other one pass. I hated it. I wanted to be close, touching, cemented together.

She nodded. "I was out, and thought I would like to see Chantilly. She's been on my mind."

"Come in." I finally got my head together and beckoned her through the door. "Want something to drink? Eat?"

She shook her head. "No, thanks. Sammy and I were out walking, and I saw a woman go into the Fritz. Dressed to the nines in the middle of the afternoon, big tote on her shoulder, and I knew the score. Made me think of Chantilly, how she's getting along." She leaned on the arm of the couch, and I stood guard in front of her.

"Lisa . . ." I used Chantilly's real name and Lynx nodded, letting me know she knew who I meant, "is good. Figuring shit out."

"She doesn't have the same number. Do you have the new one?"

"Yeah." I snagged my phone off the desk. "Let's call her and go see her."

"But you're working."

"Nothing Staci can't handle. Plus, I have to go check on the hotel."

"I haven't seen it yet, the hotel."

"One sec." I held up a finger, my phone to my ear. "Hey, Lisa. How ya doing?"

I listened as she rattled on for a moment about getting her paperwork in order. I'd offered her a job at reception in the hotel.

"Sounds great. Listen, Lynx is here and she wants to see you. Can we swing by?"

Lisa explained she was running out to pick up her daughter, but then would be back home waiting for us.

"Perfect. See you then," I said, and disconnected the call.

"Come on." I grabbed Lynx's hand out of habit. "I'll show you the hotel, and then we'll go see Lisa."

Another small smile formed and then it was gone. Lynx tried to tug her hand from mine when my thumb brushed over a few rough scabs. I stopped dead in my tracks and turned her palm up. Right there, all along the inside of her hand, were small crescent-shaped scars, along with fresher scabs.

"Don't," she said sharply in a warning tone.

"Babe." I brought her hand to my mouth and kissed each scar, every wound, taking my time, keeping a firm grip on her wrist. "We're going to make it better."

She didn't respond, but she didn't pull her hand away.

THANK YOU," Lynx whispered. She leaned her head back against the headrest after we got into my car, still parked in front of Lisa's house. "She looks good. Thank you for helping her to get out, get a life. Means a lot. I wish I could do it too, for more women."

Understanding what she meant, I nodded. "She was all I had when you disappeared. I looked after her as much as she looked after me. She worried about you almost as much as I did. Now Asher and I are taking care of her. It's what we do."

"What's with Asher? Does he think he can save the whole world?" Lynx turned her profile to me, the setting sun streaming in the window setting her skin aglow.

"Not the whole world, but he's got a soft spot for anyone who reminds him of Natalie. Hard life, even harder time getting out of a rough patch, doing shit on her own. He didn't know this about himself when he helped Lila. He just thought he was a good guy disguised as a bad one, but I guess he does now. He's touched so many lives." Amazed, I shook my head. "Listen to me. I'm a regular Oprah."

I laughed for probably the first time in months, my breath coming easily, not in ragged spurts.

Lynx laughed with me, and hearing that was worth making a fool of myself. Her giggle, soft and full of lightness, blanketed the car in her sexy aura.

"You too. He helped you too, Michael."

I nodded. "In a different way. I needed a dose of real life, away from prep schools and old Vegas money. I needed to become my own man, away from my dad and my needy mom. He helped me. I owe him everything."

"You did him proud, especially now with this hotel project. You're like no man I've ever met."

At that, I shook my head. "Smoke and mirrors, babe. I'm as human as the next, just surrounded myself with good people. Like you're doing."

"Not to me. To me, you're more."

I gave her a big smile. "I guess that's lucky for me."

"Thank you for waiting for me. Believing in me."

"It wasn't hard. You're all I've ever wanted, Lynx."

The words were there, in my heart, painted on my soul, but I didn't know if she was ready to hear them again.

Fuck it.

I turned all the way in my seat, taking her hand in mine. "I love you."

At first, she stared straight ahead, nodding. To what, I didn't know.

"I love you too, Michael." It was barely a whisper, but I heard it all the way to my shoes and back. "But I can't make promises. I wake up every morning, unsure if I love myself. Most days, I don't."

"L—"

Suddenly fierce, Lynx held up a hand. "No, don't pacify me or make promises or swear this or that. I need to love myself every morning in order to love you the way you deserve to be loved. I'm going to try. That's the best I can do."

twenty-four

LYNX WASN'T sure she could do this thing with Mike—unconditional love—but she also didn't want to go home.

Except, she didn't know how or whether to say it or not.

She also needed to check in with Sammy, but she couldn't stop rolling Mike's words around in her head.

I love you, Lynx.

She didn't deserve those words, but she was taking them, absorbing them, wrapping her soul in them. She repeated them, making promises to him to try to get her shit together.

She'd decided earlier today she would accept Michael's love and affection. After all, she craved it like potato chips and ice cream when she was PMSing. She went to him, unannounced, carrying a stupid excuse to see him like an extra suitcase at the airport.

And now, she didn't want to ever leave him.

It didn't make any sense that he wanted her, but she wanted him, so she was taking him. Keeping him.

I love you, Lynx.

"I'm not ready to let you go today, not yet," Mike said as they pulled away from the curb. "I don't want to take you home." He had her hand in his and ran his fingers through hers, not asking about the scabs or cuts anymore.

He let them be—for her.

"I don't want to go home." The words bubbled up in her throat, almost getting stuck, but she pushed them out.

He gave her a single nod and drove the car, no further words passing between them.

Lynx didn't know where he was going, but for the first time in what felt like decades, she allowed someone else to think for her.

When Mike pulled into the garage of an apartment building, she asked, "Is this where you live now?"

He nodded. "Couldn't stand staying in Asher's house after you left. Needed a place devoid of you, of memories of us. Anyway, now that house is better with Lisa filling it up with good times."

Lynx swallowed a lump in her throat at the thought that she'd abandoned him. "I wish I hadn't left you, but Sammy . . . she was all I could think about. I had a real live sister somewhere out there."

"No more regrets," he demanded. "Speaking of which, you should text her. Won't she worry?"

"Yeah. I should."

"Come on. You can send her a text when we get upstairs."

Mike got out of the SUV and opened her door, then led her to an elevator bank. When they got inside, he pushed twelve and off they went, her shoulder brushing his arm, tiny sparks igniting.

There were only two apartments on the twelfth floor. Mike's was the one on the left, a huge daunting wooden door separating his personal space from the hall. To the right of the door was a keypad where he stroked in a code.

"It's your old phone number, in case you need to use it," he said softly as a click echoed through the hall.

When the door opened, half a floor of Miami's finest views came into view.

Lynx walked straight to the windows and stared out at the city before her. She'd come here to help Natalie and to escape Vegas. She'd found her sister and set about being a hero, but in the process, she'd messed up the one thing, the *only* thing, that mattered.

Not a thing, a person.

Michael.

"Text Sammy," he reminded her, and when she did, the response was quick.

tinged

Sammy: Good for you. Thank GOD.

With her palm to the glass and her eyes trained on the city in front of her, Lynx asked, "Will you ever forgive me?" A cloak of shame fell over her shoulders, dragging her down. She felt like she carried the weight of seventeen men.

Mike came up behind her and wrapped an arm around her waist, holding her close.

"It's not even a question." He pulled back her hair and ran his mouth along her neck, sucking, nipping, loving. "What happened to your braids," he asked, his voice hoarse with need.

"Decided on a new look."

"I like it, but your braids . . . I miss them." His teeth dragged over her ear, latching onto her earlobe. "I want you so fucking bad. All of you." He squeezed her hip from behind.

Lynx twisted in his arms so she could face him, and stood on the balls of her feet to reach his mouth. "All of me?" Her lips tickled against his as she spoke.

"Every inch—past, present, and future."

And then he latched onto her mouth. He wasn't gentle. He was convincing, taking, grabbing her bottom lip between his and sucking.

A small moan came from Lynx, giving Mike's tongue entry into her mouth. With her back pressed firmly against the glass, he made love to her mouth, one hand planted on her hip, the other on her ass.

Lynx craved more friction, but she didn't want to rush this moment. It was too special, too momentous, too overwhelming with sensations.

Mike slowed and pulled his mouth away. "Is this okay?"

She nodded and ran her hand down his arm—noting the goose bumps that formed along her way.

On Big Mike.

"I want you," he said. "Think I said that already, but I can't help myself. I could say it all fucking night, but I don't want to pressure you."

Mike looked deep in her eyes, searching for an answer, maybe a commitment. She gave one quick nod and he picked her up off the floor, smiling when she wrapped her legs around his middle. He walked with her somewhere. The bedroom, she guessed.

His bedroom was decorated in white and gray, with a platform king-sized bed covered with a gray comforter. A steel dresser and bureau, and nothing else. The room was impersonal and completely devoid of any color.

Mike set her on the bed and pulled her shirt off. "There now, the place is a little brighter," he said, eyeing her red bikini top—a splash of color in the neutral room. He must have read her mind about the space.

He toed off his basketball shoes and ripped off his shirt, then lay down next to her. His hand smoothed over her belly, his index finger tracing her navel. Lynx noted the difference in their skin tones—his white to her soft brown. It never bothered her before, but after Zayid and his obsession with skin color, she wondered.

"Does it bother you? My skin?"

Mike's hand stilled. "Say what?"

"With the hotel and everything, you're going legit, making a name and all that. What will your parents say? Vegas royalty and a biracial chick?"

"Lynx, I've never loved anyone the way I've loved you. All of you. I don't care if you're red, blue, orange, or purple." His words came in puffs against her cheek. Then he rolled on top of her, keeping his weight on his elbow. "You're so gorgeous."

Kissing her deeply, he let his hand wander up and down her side, dipping his thumb into her jeans until he stopped, bent, and shimmied them off with her Chucks. Making quick work of his jeans and boxers, they were skin to skin except for Lynx's bikini top and thong.

Mike knelt over her, his knees on either side of hers, his hand running up and down the inside of her thighs. His finger swirled over her panties. When he found they were soaked, he moaned and dipped his finger beneath them, running over her bare mound. He rubbed her most sensitive spot, and she came alive.

Lynx closed her eyes and allowed herself to feel every sensation, each pulse and touch. Mike's teeth moved her top out of the way and closed over one nipple, his hand never leaving her core until she came, reaching a height she thought she'd never see again.

Then he was sheathed and inside her, her thong and bikini top tossed to the floor. He started slow and gentle, then he went fast and hard, her leg hooked over his hip, until the only word they knew was each other's names.

twenty-five

I LAY THERE with my eyes wide open, afraid to close them, terrified that Lynx would disappear again. She was sleeping in my arms, snuggled into my side, soft and naked, her tattoo on display, and I couldn't stop watching her breathing. Her rib cage rose and fell, and my gaze lingered on each movement as if my very next breath depended on it.

I kissed the top of her head, letting my lips linger one beat, then two. I had to make this work. We both had shit in our pasts we wanted to forget, and it was time to push forward.

It was up to me to make it all happen.

"Hey." Lynx stirred in my arms. "What time is it?"

"About midnight."

"Wow, I should go." She propped herself up on one arm.

"Don't."

I expected a fight, braced myself for her grabbing her clothes, calling a cab, tossing my love back in my face.

"Okay," was all she said before she settled back into my arms.

Okay.

It was only minutes before Lynx was fast asleep again, her body warm and still pressed against mine. At some point, I dozed next to her, falling into the best sleep I'd had in a long time.

L YNX WAS in my shower. *In my shower!*
It was surreal.

I was making breakfast when her phone rang in her bag. A chill ran down my spine, remembering the days when Bruno would call and she would give in to his demands. Pushing any negative thoughts to the back of my mind, I focused on making coffee, resisting the urge to look at her phone.

It wasn't easy, especially when I also had to tamp down a strong desire to join her in the shower. We'd made love the night before, but she was skittish when she woke up—and I didn't push. She was here, and that was enough for now.

"Morning." Her voice rang through my kitchen and then she appeared, wearing her clothes from yesterday, her hair on top of her head in a messy bun.

"Coffee?"

"Yeah, that'd be nice."

Coffee in hand, I approached with caution. "You good?"

She nodded, accepting the steaming mug. Jealous, I watched her lips wrap around the lip of the mug, wishing they were pressed to mine. She took a sip and set it on the counter next to her.

"What's wrong?" I stepped close, but stopped short of touching her.

She stared at my bare feet and then closed her eyes. "Did we make a mistake?"

"No, not even a little one. This is a good thing. A very good fucking thing."

"You want me? This?"

Now I bridged the gap, my hardness connecting with her curves, making sure there were zero loopholes in my words. "More than anything in the world. No hesitation."

My lips met with her forehead, and I placed a chaste kiss there. "No hesitation at all," I repeated, then picked up her mug and put it back in her hands. "Drink your coffee."

"I'd like to see your hotel in broad daylight. The Firefly, right?"

I nodded. "Then we'll do that."

She took another sip of her coffee, keeping her eyes trained on me.

"Oh, your phone rang," I told her.

She rummaged through her bag and pulled out her phone. When she murmured "Nat" as she checked the screen, I let a thousand bad thoughts go on a deep exhale.

"You can call her back if you want. I'm going to grab a shower."

Lynx nodded but was quiet, seeming to be taking in her surroundings.

"Want to go out there?" I asked.

"The balcony?"

I nodded.

"I think so. I love how the windows are wide open, no drapes."

"I didn't really give it any thought, but thanks. Come on."

I opened the door and pulled out a chair for her. Ocean air surrounded us, and a hundred memories washed over me of the night we met on the balcony in Vegas. I'd wanted to be her knight in shining armor even back then.

A chill ran down my spine as I walked back into the air-conditioning to give Lynx some space.

Could I pull it off?

I WALKED THROUGH the balcony doors a while later and took in the beauty in front of me . . . and I don't mean the water. Lynx was lying back in the chair, large sunglasses over her eyes, the sun beating down on her face.

"Natalie good?" I asked.

"She's coming to visit. Wants to take me to some frou-frou shrink. Thinks I need to talk to someone, and she's pulling the *I'm practically your mom* card."

"Do you think it would help?" I asked, all innocent as I sat down next to her. *Hey, I went to prep school; I'm not all hood. I know a bit about reverse psychology.*

"I don't want to talk."

"Sometimes it may help. I don't know." Leaning forward in my chair, I took her hands in mine.

"I want to close the door, not reopen it. I feel like all that talking is like cutting fresh wounds."

I raised an eyebrow. "Isn't that sort of happening anyway?" I asked, hinting at the cuts on her palm without saying the words.

She shrugged without looking me in the eye.

"Is Sammy talking to someone?"

She nodded.

"Does it seem to be helping?"

Another shrug.

"How about we actually talk and not only nod and shrug," I said, calling her out. "I'm here for you, so let's discuss it. Maybe you'll give it a try and see? It could help, plus Nat's coming all this way."

"Maybe." She squeezed my hand, and I held hers tighter. "Just maybe. I don't know."

At least she was talking.

"Is Ash coming? The kids? I can't see him not checking out the Firefly." I got a smile and a sparkle in her eyes with that question.

"The whole gang is coming, so I'll meet the twins and see Quinney. God, he's going to be so big."

"Turning into a nice young man. That's why Asher wanted the hotel. Wants to give him something a hundred percent legit. If this works out, we're going to build another. Boutique luxury experiences, private, secluded. Not huge enormous monstrosities, but smaller, catering to people's whims."

"I hope Quinney remembers me."

It was awesome to see her face light up when talking about Quinn.

"Babe, no one could ever forget you. Even a scrawny kid you used to babysit."

Another smile and sparkle from her made my heart swell.

Winning.

twenty-six

A SHER SLAPPED me on the back. "You done good, Mike."
"I thought you were all worried," I said with a grin, puffing on my cigar.

We sat around a makeshift desk on what would be the patio outside my office at the Firefly, Asher in his motorcycle boots and me in my basketball shoes—a pair not to be messed with on any day. Fucking right I was going to have a mack-daddy office . . . I'd worked hard as shit for it.

"For a while there, I was," Asher said. "Now that you got the girl back where you want her, don't push her, Mike. Don't rush her."

"Because you know how to do that so well?"

"I never said to do what I did. I'm an idiot. A rich one, thank fuck for that. The hotel is fucking perfect, so you know what I say?"

"Hmm?"

He stared me down with his silver eyes, his cigar burning between two fingers. "Don't fuck it up. Don't fucking fuck up anything."

"Copy, sir," I said, earning myself a smack on the back of my head.

"Cut your fucking hair too. I'm the only one with good hair around here."

I lifted my cigar to my mouth. "I plan to when I get my lady back for good."

L ATER THAT evening, Asher being Asher, he arranged for some private catered dinner on the Firefly property, specifically where the pool deck was currently being built. Our Miami Wave gang and Asher's family were seated around one big table lit by tea-light candles—Natalie's soft touch. After a small rundown of dates, announcements, thanks, and toasts, Asher shared the hotel's official opening date and some other big news.

"It came as a bit of surprise with a teen boy and twin toddlers, but I guess we're just that good. Nat and I are having a baby." He raised his glass and winked at his wife. "Just one baby this time, not two. My swimmers are good, but not that good. Plus, I'm getting old." He ran a hand through his thick hair. "Eh, I guess not that old."

The guy was so fucking in love with himself, but not nearly as much as he loved his family.

I wanted that. All of it.

As congratulations rang out from around the table, the need to squeeze Lynx's hand or thigh ran through me, coursing through my veins, but I couldn't. She'd intentionally sat across from me, her eyes on Asher and Natalie kissing and hanging on to each other as if their last breath depended on it.

Asher mouthed *love you, doll* and kissed his wife again. Staci was crying at the sight; she'd been in Vegas when Asher and Natalie finally ended their decade-long separation.

My gaze returned to Lynx, noting her glassy eyes and how she sniffed back tears. We'd been seeing each other about every other day for the last two weeks—a meal here and there, a cup of coffee, a run, but that was it—since she'd spent that one glorious night with me.

I wasn't pushing or complaining. I wanted more, but in due time.

Natalie arrived a few days ago, and had been pushing Lynx to see a new therapist. I didn't know who or what or where or when, and when I'd asked Natalie about it, she told me, "Talk to the hand, Big Mike. I got the deets from Carson. You stay out of it, way out."

I didn't have any other choice. Those women were batshit crazy.

I'd never guessed Lynx would refuse to sit next to me tonight, though. Before I even knew what I was doing, I got up from the table and rounded it, stopping on the other side.

"Get up," I told Sampson.

tinged

"The fuck?"

"Get up, dude. I want to sit here with Lynx."

Lynx frowned up at me. "Mike, don't do this."

"Michael," I said, correcting her.

"*Michael.*"

To me, it was a whisper, a prayer, a beckoning—not a warning like she meant it to be.

"Move, for the last time," I told Sampson, and he did. After all, I was his boss.

I slid into his chair and smoothed my hand down Lynx's bare arm. A shiver ran through her, and I all too willingly absorbed it. When she looked at me, I pressed my lips to her forehead, marking her in front of everyone watching us.

That's right, they should know. I was laying claim for good.

"You want a baby, Lynx?" It was a whisper, soft enough for only her to hear. When she closed her eyes, I traced the small furrow in her brow with my lips. "I want you to have my babies. One or ten, I don't care, I just want it with you."

"What if I don't deserve them? Babies." She leaned in, whispering in my ear.

"You do. You need to see someone, get over this. Nat has me all cock-blocked, keeping me at arm's length, and I fucking hate it. Then you don't sit next to me. I want to know what's going on," I said, my whisper more of a growl. "I want in, all the way in."

My lips sought Lynx's, and I kissed the fuck out of her. If she would have told me to stop, I would have, but she didn't. So I kissed her.

Vaguely, I heard a catcall and a whistle. These were our friends, our family, so who cared? Not me.

"Lynx," I said softly. "I'll do anything to help you get over this, climb this mountain."

"Michael." This time when she breathed my name, it wasn't meant to be a deterrent. It was a salve.

"Want to get out of here?"

She nodded.

Grabbing her hand, I stood from the table and gave everyone a quick wave. "We're out."

Natalie waved back. "Lynx, don't forget we're taking the twins to the playground in the morning. Quinney is going to go to work with Ash and Mike."

"Quinn," the young buck growled at her from next to his father.

With a smile like a cat that ate all the cream, Natalie turned back to her conversation. She didn't care what any of those alpha brutes said; she did what she wanted. We'd all learned that a long time ago.

As for tonight, the little vixen set me up. Pushed my buttons by keeping me in the dark when it came to Lynx, tossing me right into the open flames.

"The place is really turning out gorgeous." Lynx squeezed my hand as we walked through the almost complete lobby. Soon we would start bringing in a few travel experts to get a glimpse of the Firefly.

"I never thought I'd go into the hotel biz, but I guess it's in my blood."

"That's not a bad thing. You can be like your dad when it comes to business."

"Not entirely like him. I want to add my own touch. See things the way I see them. As for the personal stuff, we can't ever really be family," I told her. "I never wanted to do what he did—tear my family apart, make my kid feel unwanted, and walk away unmarked."

"You could never. Your heart is way too big. That's why they call you Big Mike."

"You mean it's not for my muscles?"

This got me the full-on smile, a laugh, and a punch in the arm. I'd take another.

"Where do you want to go?" I asked as we stood in the circular driveway, my convertible out front.

"Can we take a ride?"

"Yep, let's go."

Opening the door for her, I watched Lynx slide into my BMW and remembered all the nights I'd driven around, endlessly looking for her.

She was here now, and I planned to keep it that way.

After jumping in the driver's seat, I pressed the gas pedal and we sped out. My hand worked the manual shift, and for the first time, I was pissed I didn't buy the automatic.

I drove north to Miami Beach, past all the luxury hotels, and pulled over at the end of the strip. When I lowered the top, the ocean air surrounded us in its salt and humidity, and I took in the beauty in front of me.

"Can I kiss you again?"

"Oh, now you're asking permission?"

"Nope." I leaned across the console and took her lips in mine. On a soft exhale, our tongues twisted, and I slid my hand behind her neck and underneath her braids.

Squeezing gently, I massaged the tension from Lynx's neck and swallowed all of her moans. It was perfect. I could have stayed here all night like this, but she pulled away.

"You okay?"

She nodded and brought her hand to my face, running the back of it down my cheek. I gently took her wrist and turned her palm toward my skin.

"You don't have to hide anything from me," I said, my hushed tone swallowed by the night.

Lynx closed her eyes and whispered, "I'm going to see that person Nat wants me to see."

I nodded, trying hard to contain my excitement. After years as a bouncer, I could do calm and collected.

"I want to try," she said, opening her eyes to look at me with so much emotion, it nearly stopped my heart. "You, me, us. Slow. I don't want you to be in the dark. It's just hard."

Another nod from me.

We'd already had several rounds of the same question, but I didn't push. I knew better than to do that; the only thing I could do was bide my time. But I could tell she wasn't finished talking.

Lynx gave me a sad smile. "But I need to take the lead. For years, everything was so out of my control. I know it was my choice, my doing, but now I want to be in control. See someone, take charge of the bad feelings, get a job, all that."

"I'm by your side, however you want. You're in charge."

I was getting my girl back. My woman. On her terms, but she was back.

"I want a job," she said. "At the club."

This time, I shook my head.

"I need to get out of my place, doing too much sitting around. I also need to feel safe. I want to work there . . . because you're there."

"Lynx . . ." When she put it that way, what could I say? "Staci's running the club more and more, and I'm going to be at the hotel soon. I don't want you at the Wave. Too much past crap and bullshit all wrapped up there. It's not a bad place. Believe me, I run a classy joint, but no. Just no."

"So, the hotel. I can help there. I'm already in love with the place."

Hmm. That idea had legs.

"What about marketing?" I asked. "Or giving tours to travel

people?"

She bit her lower lip. "I thought bartending?"

"No, babe. Not bartending." I bit down a laugh I didn't think she would appreciate.

"You sure?"

"As sure as my name is Michael Anthony Wind, and I was apparently born for the hotel biz."

"Okay, so can I start doing something soon?"

"If it means I can see more of you, hell yes."

"I need to stay busy, and whether I want to admit it or not, I don't always feel safe unless you're around."

"I'm not going anywhere."

"Can we kiss again?"

"Hell yeah." And I was back across the console.

twenty-seven

LYNX MET Natalie at the park the following day, and watched with equal parts pride and envy as Natalie played with the twins. They were adorable, Lillie dressed in a white tank and a pink tutu, and Parker clad in tiny jeans and a white T-shirt—like a mini Nat and Asher.

Want and need burned in Lynx's belly. She'd never had a normal family life growing up, never imagined being a parent one day, but suddenly it didn't seem so far-fetched. Maybe one day she could?

"I'm so glad you're going to see someone," Natalie said as she pushed Parker in the swing.

"It's time, I guess. I've been moping around here. Even Sammy is doing better than me. I need to pull my life together once and for all, stop lying to myself that I'm okay, and stop ruining the lives of everyone around me." Lynx pushed Lillie, the desire to have her own child raging. Lillie's hair blew in the wind, taking flight with every push.

How did Michael know these private thoughts of hers? It was like they were meant for each other.

"Aw, honey, don't think that. You don't ruin anything."

"Look at how I lied to you in the beginning about what I was really doing. And what about how Mike learned about Quinn? All of it, it was messed up back in Vegas, and then I made it all worse down here."

"You didn't. I know it. You did what you thought was right. This is why I'm so glad you're going to see the doctor."

"Higher," Parker yelled.

"Okay, you little daredevil. Just like your dad, my big, bad boy."

"Make it higher!"

Natalie pushed the swing a little higher, and Parker pumped his short legs. "How's Mike? He's being patient?"

"More than I deserve."

"Lynx, I've known you a long time now, trusted my own child with you back in the day. You deserve the world. Stop with all this negative talk. You're too good for that."

She shrugged. Some days she agreed, others she didn't.

"One day, this'll be you. A bunch of kids. Mike taking care of you and them. He'll be a great dad."

"I was just thinking about that earlier. It's like my thoughts are playing out on my face these days."

"I could tell. You had this far-off, rosy-cheeked look. I know the look, honey."

"Oh, please . . ."

"Oh, please, nothing. Come on, let's take these monkeys to the coffee shop."

L YNX TEXTED Mike when she was finished with coffee.

> *Lynx: I'm done with Nat. Want to walk thru hotel?*

A few minutes later, the little bubble with three dots appeared on her phone.

> *Mike: Almost done with Ash. Quinn wants to come with us. Cool with you?*

Lynx hadn't spent much time with Quinn since she'd left Vegas. She worried he knew what she'd done for a living. For some reason, she wanted to remain pure and good in his eyes.

> *Lynx: Are you sure? I can do it later?*

This time, the bubble with the three dots came immediately.

tinged

Mike: Babe, 110% sure. Come now. Quinn loves you.

He could read her thoughts. There was no other explanation.

Taking a deep breath, Lynx went to her car and took a moment or two behind the wheel. Tomorrow, she had an appointment with Dr. Jensen. She could do this, paint herself a new color. A bright one—yellow like the sun, or bright orange like the horizon.

A happy color.

twenty-eight

'M HERE. *Parking.*

I texted Lynx from downstairs, giving her time to prepare before seeing me. I knew better than to think she was ready for this. She was making me dinner at her place the day after her first appointment.

I didn't expect her to go into a lot of detail about her session, but I wanted her to relax and be comfortable with me. Last night, she'd stayed home with Sammy, and I assumed they'd discussed what they needed to. Their relationship was at the core of this, and needed as much repair as Lynx and mine.

I buzzed at the front entrance, and one of them let me in. When I got to their condo, Lynx's sister greeted me at the door.

"Hey, I'm Sammy. I know we met once, but still."

"Mike." I winked. We'd met when the two sisters first came back to the States. Landon was the hero then, but that wasn't a happy occasion for anyone.

"Want to come in?"

"You bet."

She stepped to the side and made room for me to come in. "Lynx is cooking, and I'm on tasting duty."

"Sounds like an important job."

She laughed. It was soft, not as full-bodied as Lynx's laugh, but it was all Sammy.

I could tell they were sisters—their faces were remarkably similar. Must have been from their dad. But their bodies told the story of two different moms. Sammy's frame was slight and less curvy, like her laugh.

I guess I was a full-bodied type of guy.

"Smells good in here," I hollered, walking into the entryway. I hadn't seen the inside yet, but it was your standard oceanfront condo.

"Hey." Lynx stood in the kitchen wearing jeans cutoffs, a red tank, her hair on top of her head, no makeup, and barefoot.

I fell in love—all over again—in that moment. I imagined coming home every day to this. Of course, she didn't have to cook, just be herself, pure and good.

"You hungry?"

I walked up to her, snatching her around the waist and pulling her close. "I am. Very."

She stood on tiptoe to whisper in my ear. "For food?"

"Oh yeah, I am." Pinching her side, I stepped back.

"I'm making tamales. Want a beer? Or something stronger?"

"Point me in the right direction and I'll get it. Sammy eating with us?"

"Is that okay?"

"I was hoping."

This got me another one of those big smiles. Huge, in fact.

"Where's the drinks?"

"Right here," Sammy said from behind me, standing next to a small wet bar. Of course, Asher spared no expense in setting up these two. They never worked for the Tunnel, but Lynx had babysat Quinn long before Asher knew he had a son. She was golden to him.

"Slide over," I told Sammy. "What's your poison?"

"Vodka and soda."

I nodded and got to work. "Lynx, babe?"

She looked up from the stove and took my breath away. Christ, I was having some sort of out-of-body experience, watching my future life pass before my eyes, or some crazy, whacked-out shit like that.

"Wine, white."

I grabbed a bottle of wine from the hidden mini-fridge and poured a glass before making Sammy her drink. Then I tossed two fingers of

Jack into a lowball and said, "Cheers, ladies."

"Cheers," Sammy called out.

Lynx took a sip of her wine, and I pretended not to see how her eyes glistened.

Nodding my approval, I looked around me. "I like the place."

"It's home for now," Sammy said. "But soon, I'm going to head toward Lauderdale. I like that Las Olas area, the boutiques and stuff. I'm going to try and open one, sell handmade accessories . . . Jeez, I'm sorry. I'm rambling."

"Hey, that's awesome."

"And Landon's up there," Lynx called out from the kitchen.

Sammy blushed. "Not all the time. He still travels for work. But you know, I got that whole Stockholm thing going, or whatever you call it. He rescued me, so maybe it's not that. I'm just kind of infatuated with him."

Lynx turned and grinned at her. "Sam, you're still rambling."

"Ha, I know. Tell Mike what happened today."

"It's not a big deal."

Giving Lynx a pointed look, I said, "Try me."

"I've been keeping a diary of all that happened, and Sammy got a wild hair to share it with some publishing guy she met at the bar. He offered me a book deal to write about what went down over there."

I tossed back the rest of my drink, the burn taking away my trepidation. "You sure you want to?"

"At first I didn't, but Sammy and I chatted about it. I went back again today to the shrink . . . two days in a row . . . look at me! She thinks it may be cathartic to help others, to teach or whatever."

I lifted my drink to Lynx in a toast. "I'm behind you no matter what."

"We'll see. I still don't know if that's my calling. Plus, I'm going to be busy with tours for the hotel."

"Babe, those tours can wait."

"I need that job, Mike."

"Want to eat on the balcony?" Sammy called from in front of the TV.

"Yes, so you get away from the news," Lynx called back.

"Just taking a quick peek."

"What can I do?" I asked, closing in on Lynx in the kitchen.

"Take Sammy outside. She's not supposed to obsess over CNN. The world is still standing . . . that's all she needs to know. I'll bring the food out."

"Ten-four, boss."

I headed over to Sammy, my basketball shoes sinking into the plush carpet. Asher set these ladies up, which should make me happy, but I'd rather it had been me. I made a mental note to start taking over shit when it came to these two.

"Come on. Your sister wants us to go outside and wait."

Sammy rolled her eyes before she flicked off the TV and opened the sliding door.

"Where you tending bar?" I sat in a lounger, leaning back and breathing deep.

"Primo Steak on First." Sammy sat at the table, resting her chin in the palm of her hand.

"Nice place. You like it?"

"It's the kind of place you go to if you've been in *People* magazine or read it. It's a see-and-be-seen kind of joint. Big crowds means big tips, so yeah, I like it."

"You want to get out, though? Do your crafting?"

"Jewelry making," she said, correcting me.

"You should do that. You need a backer?"

Her laugh filled the air. "I didn't know where you were going with all this, but I get it now. You think if I stay legit, there's a better chance that Lynx doesn't get sucked back into shit."

"I do. I'm not denying it. I lived with her shit for a long time, played second fiddle to whatever negative notions she had about herself, and then her mission to find you. Now she did, and I want her to myself."

Samara shook her head. "I admit it's a noble cause, but I don't need a backer. I got money in the bank, just didn't want to leave L until she got her shit together. Now that she's seeing someone and decided to trust you again, I'm close to getting out."

I leaned forward. "Appreciate you doing that. Staying here, waiting for Lynx to come around."

"She's my sister. Trekked to the other side of the goddamn earth for me, burdened herself with a lifetime of crap memories for me."

I nodded. "They're all going to be good from now on."

"From your mouth to God's ears, Big Mike. You have his cell number?"

We were both laughing when Lynx appeared with a huge platter of food. Jumping from the lounger, I ran over to help, sliding my hand over Lynx's ass and giving it a pinch. Her answering grin made it all worthwhile.

"You both want water?" I asked, and when they nodded, I went in and grabbed three bottles from the fridge.

Seated around the table, the three of us chowed down until Sammy got a call from Landon. When she bounded like a puppy on speed into the condo, Lynx and I stayed outside to give her some privacy. The food all gone, we relaxed at the table, enjoying the sound of the surf and the darkening sky.

"What are you going to do when Sammy heads to Lauderdale?" I was full of tamales and myself, blurting out my thoughts to Lynx when I should have been doing dishes. We sat across from each other, the table a nuisance, keeping us too far apart.

"Stay here in Miami. I'm not going to go with her. She's chasing Landon."

"You mean here by yourself?"

"I haven't thought about that. I've lived by myself before. I even had my own apartment over—"

"I didn't mean you couldn't." Taking her hands in mine and resting them on the table, I said, "I meant you could move in with me."

"Michael . . ." Her smaller hand squeezed my large one. "One thing my therapist said is you need to be able to hear about what happened. It's a part of my story. You can't interrupt me or shush me every time I mention it."

Shit.

For lack of any reply, I cleared my throat. "It's because I want to leave it there. In your past. In a different world, one where you don't exist anymore."

"Me too." She stood and came around to take Sammy's vacant seat. "But we have to acknowledge it happened."

"If that's what we need to do, we'll do it."

As I spoke, she brought the back of her hand to my cheek and caressed my stubble.

Why was she comforting me? I was supposed to be the big brute.

Without thinking, I turned her hand, wanting to feel the coarseness of her scabs, needing to remind myself she'd been through hell. "Did you show them to her? Shit, I promised myself I wouldn't ask a bunch of crap. I'd let you tell me."

Her hand stilled on my cheek.

"I showed her. She wants to help me stop. She thinks talking will help, let some of the pain out of me rather than me doing this."

"Good." Grabbing her hand, I placed my lips over her knuckles, pressing kisses all over.

"Do you still love me?"

"More," I said. "That's why I want you to move in with me, which you never answered."

"Do you think that's smart?"

"I think it's pure genius."

twenty-nine

A FEW WEEKS turned into a month. Staci officially moved into my office at the Wave, and I moved into my posh new one at the Firefly. I still checked in on the club every day, but Staci knew what she was doing. Let's face it—I trained her right.

I was putting away some shit in my private bathroom at the Firefly when my phone rang.

"Mike?"

"You got me. What's up, Sammy?"

"I got a lease up in Las Olas for the store, right next to a Brazilian food place. It's perfect."

"Sounds good. What do you need from me? Told you I'd back you." I stepped out onto my patio, hidden by palm trees from the outdoor spaces of the hotel.

"I'm going to move. Soon, maybe this weekend. Landon offered me a room at his place, and, well, I want to give it a try."

I nodded, even though she couldn't see. "Lynx know?" When the line remained silent, I said, "Sammy, I'm not telling her."

"Mike, come on. She's working hard. I don't want to be the one to break her heart."

tinged

I paced the small patio. "I already asked her twice to move in with me, and both times it's been a big fat no. She'll have to stay at your place alone until she decides she wants me full-time."

Sammy sighed. "I'm sorry."

"It's not your fault. I'm being patient . . . as patient as a man can be, taking scraps."

"I'll tell her. Maybe she'll come running to you."

"Doubtful, but a man can dream."

"You're a good one, Big Mike. Glad I have you."

"You got me, babe. You and your sister."

She ended the call, and I went back into my office and sat down at my desk. Everything was so fucking plush. Leather and glass. I wasn't in a strip club anymore, Toto.

My phone rang again, and it was Asher about the opening-night party. It was going to be some huge fussed-about deal, splashed on the society pages. Every shmuck in Miami was coming, my parents included. Separately, of course.

Lila was staying back and taking care of the Los Angeles club so Petey, Asher's half brother, could come. It was meant to be a family affair, and Lila wanted that for Asher, even though he considered her family.

Lynx was giving me shit about my insisting she come too, but for this, I wasn't taking no for an answer. My woman was going to be on my arm for this event.

O N MY way home, I popped into the Wave to have a drink with Sampson. I was going to miss my bouncers. They felt like the brothers I never had growing up.

Seated at the main bar, he tossed back a rum and Coke. I was nursing a Jack straight up when I heard Jovi call my name. Lynx was by his side, good and pissed.

She stomped over to me. "Did you tell Sammy to move? So I would move in with you?"

"What? No fucking way."

Sampson slid his empty glass toward the bartender. "I'm out. Good seeing you, man."

"Sit down," I said calmly, then asked Lynx, "Want a drink?"

"No, I want an answer. I've been doing everything that everyone wants."

"Hey, no one is pressuring you. I told you to do anything and

133

everything you wanted or needed," I said, tossing her words back at her. "Sammy wants to move, be with this guy, start a new life. You're still going to be a part of it."

Her gaze focused on my shoes, and I tipped her chin up. "You have a big family now. Me. Sammy. I'm guessing even Landon. Plus, the Tunnel gang."

"Mike—" Just as she was about to speak, she looked past me and a scowl formed on her face.

"Hey, Big Mike. Lynx." Marta sashayed over, her tits and ass on display in some red strappy bodysuit.

"Hey, Mart, we're in the middle of something important." I wanted to punch myself square in the face for ever starting up with her.

"Oh, sorry. Wanted to say hi, that's it. You look good, Lynx. Love the tank," Marta said before walking away.

Lynx sucked in a breath before huffing it out. "Sometimes, I'm so pissed she helped rescue me, because I can't hate her."

I gathered Lynx in my arms and pulled her close, between my thighs. "Stop. Now, tell me what you were going to say."

"I want to move in, but I'm scared. What if it doesn't work out and I'm left with nothing?"

"Not possible." Grabbing her by the hand, I said, "Come on. Let's go to my . . . *our* place, and make it official."

There was no point in dragging out this discussion. Lynx was moving on, and moving in with me, which meant I was getting my way.

Finally.

I'D MADE it my business to know Lynx's schedule. Her routine was no secret to me when she moved in, but she didn't know that.

She went to class on Mondays, Wednesdays, and Fridays, and worked for me on Tuesdays and Thursdays. A few days a week, she had coffee with Lisa in the middle of the day. What she didn't do anymore was go to the gym.

"There's an exercise room downstairs if you want to use it," I told her as she put her stuff into drawers. It had been a week since she'd agreed to move in, and now she was here unpacking. "It's not as nice as the place you belong to, but it's cool."

Kicked back on the bed wearing only mesh shorts, with my shoes and shirt on the floor after my run, I surveyed the beauty in front of me. It was Tuesday, and we didn't have anywhere to be for a while.

I needed to hit up the club on my way to the hotel, check on payroll shit. Lynx had an appointment with the doc before coming in to the hotel. None of that started until after noon.

"Unless you're not feeling it. Working out, I mean."

Her braids fell like a drape in front of her face. "Are you saying I need to work out?"

"Nah." I laughed. "You look pretty damn perfect to me. Just wondering why you don't go anymore."

She shrugged.

"Gotta be more than that, babe."

She slammed the drawer shut and looked up at me, some of the fire I used to know her to have burning bright. "Last time I was there, I ran into Marta. Look . . . like I said, she's nice. She saved me and she saved Sammy, so I shouldn't feel this way, but you fucked her. Loved her. You still care for her, and I can't reconcile that."

There was nothing I could say. She was right. That's how the second part of our story began, Lynx and mine, with me screwing Marta. This wasn't a surprise. I knew all along it would come to bite me in the ass.

And now it was biting—like a hungry wolf.

"I can't change that. It was wrong, shitty, stupid, whatever else you want to say. I was a dick. A lonely, scared dick. But I don't ask you to change your past. I don't care because you're here now. With me. How we got here doesn't mean dick. We're here."

She leaned back into the dresser, her warm, creamy skin tone a stark contrast to the cold steel. "When I met Nat at the park and we went for coffee, she told me if we were a romance book, we'd be labeled NOT SAFE. Our story isn't for the faint at heart. Most readers would pass us over as another heartache tale. They'd call you out, label you the piece of shit they'd make you out to be with their words."

"Babe—"

She shook her head. "But she also said that her story with Asher wasn't safe either. And freaking look at them! Happy, making babies, all their dreams coming true. She said that sometimes from the worst pain, the most evil actions, happiness is born. She also said it was up to me to believe it or not; I just don't know if I can. There are so many reminders. Lisa's always asking me about over there, and Marta's at the gym, and now therapy."

"Come here," I said to her.

She shook her head.

"Come here." This time I growled.

She shook her head but walked toward me. Snatching her by the waist, I pulled her on top of me on the bed. With her thighs splayed on either side of mine, I resisted the urge to lift my hips and press myself against her. I wanted the friction, but I didn't know what she needed.

I stared deep into her troubled eyes. "Our happiness is born out of whatever we say it is. I was a piece of shit, but not anymore. You were something else back then, and now you're not. It's behind us. You have a lot on your plate. Take it easy on yourself."

"I want that happiness. I do."

I ran my hands up her side, the sheer white tank doing little to hide the heat coursing through her veins. "You're getting it."

"I don't want you to fire Marta."

"I'm not. I can't."

"I know. She risked it all for me," Lynx whispered.

"For us," I said, correcting her.

"For us." She leaned forward, resting her forehead on mine as she mumbled, "Love you."

I squeezed her tight, and her warmth lined up with my hardness. I shifted but . . . damn, I wanted to be inside her.

Her lips found mine and laid a constellation of soft kisses everywhere. She tracked her way down my jaw and over my chest, moving further, sliding off my shorts.

"I haven't showered," I choked out.

"Don't care. You're all salty, all man, all mine." She gripped me, wrapping her hand around my girth, sliding it up and down with just the right amount of pressure.

My only thought was, *Lynx is made for me.*

She brought both legs over to one side and knelt over me, bringing her mouth to my tip, her tongue fluttering out and teasing me.

"Take me, all of me," I said, my voice hoarse and needy.

And she did. Lynx took all of me, her hand remaining steady on the base, her pinky finger tracing my balls. I could have blown right there, but I was a strong believer in *ladies first*. I let her lave and suck me a while longer, closing my eyes and enjoying each ripple of sensation that made its way up and down my spine.

When I was close, I pulled her up and kissed her mouth, using one hand to push down her shorts, and found her ready for me. My fingers explored freely, eliciting moans from her until she exploded on my hand. Swallowing her moans, I turned her back to the bed, grabbed protection with one hand, and guided myself inside her.

Neither of us made it anywhere on time that day.

thirty

Two months later

Lynx sat in the wingback leather chair, her legs under her and her eyes closed. "I can't seem to allow myself to forget or to forgive."

"Lynx, it's not about forgetting," her shrink said matter-of-factly. "It doesn't even have to be about forgiving. You can hold yourself accountable. Something good came out of your transgressions. Sammy is home, safe, and near you. This is about saying it happened, putting it on a shelf, and moving on."

"What if I'm not supposed to move on?" Lynx leaned forward, the strap of her tank falling off one shoulder.

"Are you here? Breathing? Living? Talking to me?"

She nodded, shoving her hair into a knot.

"Then you're supposed to move on."

"I mentioned Marta to Mike. He feels bad. I could probably push him more on it, but I know I shouldn't."

Dr. Jensen set her pen and pad of paper onto her desk. She wore her black hair in a tight bun at her nape, a small rosary hanging around her neck. "It's clear from how you describe him, Michael wants everyone to think of him as Big Mike—strong, protective, blind to pain and suffering. But he's not. Inside, Michael is a kind human being, once

137

emotionally abandoned by his parents. Like your friend Asher you always speak about, Michael has a rescue fantasy."

"Do you think that's what I am to him?"

"No," she told Lynx point-blank. "I think you're the love of his life. Do I think what happened with Marta was smart? Probably not. But somewhere in his subconscious, he was saving another innocent young woman from the streets. Like he picked up the pieces for your friend Lisa."

Lynx nodded. She knew all this to be true, but was still was having a hard time getting over it. "I know, I know. I want to believe; that's my problem."

"If you know, you can believe. Close your eyes."

With her eyes closed again, Lynx tried to push herself to a place of belief. It was like a bright light at the end of a dark tunnel . . . she could see it but couldn't touch it.

She'd been coming to therapy for a few months now, living with Mike for two of them, and she needed to put this to bed. All the worrying, thinking, rehashing was taxing her.

"What do you see?" Dr. Jensen asked her.

"I see a life, a good one, a decent one. I want to be done with all this—no offense. Like wiping sand off my hands, I want to brush this all away."

The doctor blew out a small breath. "Tell me about the life you see."

"Michael, older, more distinguished-looking, even more successful. A house by the water, a kid, my sister with us around a fire pit, making s'mores." Lynx laughed on the last word. "You know, I've never made s'mores. I heard about them from the kids at school while growing up, and I've seen them at movies. I want my kids to make s'mores with Michael."

"That sounds like a wonderful life. It's the most natural instinct to want more for our kids than we had."

Feeling a tear slip from the corner of her eye, Lynx kept her eyes squeezed shut.

"But I have to say this," Dr. Jensen said. "What you're here for, what you did, it isn't something that can be wiped away. Look at me, Lynx."

Reluctantly, she opened her eyes.

"Your past, your mom, the decisions you made, all of those are part of you. What we need to do is shelve the negative and ground ourselves in the positive. You helped rescue your sister, and you helped shed light on this situation. Your book would serve to help others. Speaking of which, what did you decide to do about the book? I know the deadline to let them know was a few days ago."

"I want to believe that. I'm reaching for that life. But it's not easy. I have a lot of ghosts. As for the book, it's a yes. I'm doing it." Lynx finally smiled, and felt it reach her eyes. "Strange how I can be so happy about it, but I am. I feel like many tears will be shed, but the writing will help, I hope. Help others."

"I will help you. Putting your experiences and thoughts down in writing so others can learn will be cathartic, Lynx. I'm so very proud of you."

Lynx could feel herself practically glowing as happiness filled her veins.

"I understand. Listen, our work may not be done for a while, but I believe you'll be having a good life soon, long before we're finished. A deserving life, Lynx, one with meaning and purpose. When the ghosts loom too large, we need to shut them down. Not with scratching our palms and looking for blood. With talking, long walks, meditating, making love, whatever works."

"Thanks," Lynx said with a nod, praying the woman's words were true. Lynx had agreed to publish the book because she wanted good to come out of her undoing. She never wanted another young girl to be lured into sex trafficking, whether to make money or for any other reason.

"It's going to be an incredible journey," Dr. Jensen said. "I can't wait to read a first draft. So, when do you start?"

"I'm going to take a break from school. It feels like I'm too old or worldly or whatever to be there. I'll be helping Mike and writing every other moment."

"If it means anything, in my mind, you're a pioneer. We need to bathe your mind in that thought, Lynx."

Lynx digested Dr. Jensen's words. She wanted to devour them quickly, but she allowed herself time to savor each one.

Was she a pioneer?

She hoped so.

LYNX LEFT her weekly therapy appointment, and rather than going to get a cup of coffee or call Sammy, she decided to surprise Michael.

The hotel was close to opening and she knew he'd be there, alternating between Facetiming with Asher and pacing his office, talking with vendors.

Settled in her car, she pulled out of the Miami office building and headed back toward South Beach. Once she was over the bridge, she decided to park near the coffee shop and walk over to the new hotel. As she neared the Fritz on foot, she heard a familiar voice.

"Lincoln! How ya doing, babe?"

Looking up, she caught sight of Bruno leaning against a fancy red car parked at the curb. Stunned, she dropped her gaze to the sidewalk in front of her as she kept walking.

"Don't ignore me, sugar," he called out as he headed toward her. "I got a lot of calls asking me where the hell you are and when you're coming back. I figure you owe me."

Lynx kept moving, not sure what to do. People rollerbladed by the beach, seagulls flew overhead, but no one paid any attention to the biracial woman being hounded by Bruno. That's the world we lived in . . . selfish.

"I don't owe you anything," she spat out, keeping her gaze down.

"Oh, you don't?" he said, his snide voice so much closer now.

She shook her head, her gaze darting around, looking for someone who might help. *Where's a cop when you need one?*

"Talked to Zayid's guy. He wants me to send over every dark girl I have in my stable. See what you caused? More girls to go, more chaos and hurt."

Tears stung behind her eyes at his words. "You caused that. Not me, Bruno. Why don't you close up shop? Then more girls won't go. And you should leave here."

She didn't dare look at him for fear he'd sense her fear, prey on her weakness for saving others. Apparently, she and Mike weren't so different after all.

"Why's that?" Bruno asked from directly in front of her. "Pretty boy gonna come after me again? I let him take Chantilly . . . who needed her, anyway? The washed-up snitch. But I'd sure like you back."

Furious, she stopped just a foot away from Bruno and hooked a hand on her hip. The palm of her other hand made contact with his cheek, the sharp slap resonating off the buildings around them.

His eyes widened. "You bitch! Fucking whore."

Bruno brought up his hand to swing back, his fingers balled into a tight fist. He'd hit a girl many times before—Lynx had seen it.

"Not so fast, tough guy," a deep voice called out from nearby.

thirty-one

I NEEDED SOME air. I'd been on the phone all morning with Asher, and his constant grilling was getting on my nerves. He should just come out and see the hotel for himself, but Natalie was keeping him busy with supervising a teenage Quinn while she was chasing the twins and being pregnant.

I got it, though, and I owed him the respect to put up with it.

It was my dad who really pissed me off. I didn't owe the ass a damn thing. When he called and said he'd love to come out for the opening, to show me what could be managed better, I fucking lost it.

Yeah, he was the brains and brawn behind Wind Resorts, but I knew what the fuck I was doing. I'd been running a successful business for a while, and damn, Asher and I weren't copying Wind Resorts. We had our own goddamn vision.

On top of all that shit, Lynx wasn't picking up her phone. She had therapy today, and then she said she was going to hang with Lisa. Now she was fucking MIA, and for some reason, the hairs on the back of my neck were prickling.

Full of fucking nerves, I traded my jeans and Air Force 1s for running shorts and shoes. Tossing my tee on the floor, I grabbed my earbuds and went for a run. It was either that or hit a bottle of JD hard. The latter wouldn't help anybody or anyone, only my battered ego.

With rap blaring in my ears, I ran the concourse along the ocean, the sun beating on my back, zigzagging to avoid tourists and skaters. It was crowded, and I was trying to pay attention so I didn't bump into anyone, until I caught a glimpse of long black braids and legs that went for days.

Stopping dead in my tracks, I saw Lynx across the street, standing in front of the Fritz as she argued with Bruno. She had her hand on her hip, her jaw set away from him until in one quick swoop, she turned and slapped his face.

I yanked out my earbuds and hauled ass over there faster than I'd ever run, making it just in time for Bruno to raise his hand in retaliation. Fucker could call my woman names, but strike her? No fucking way.

"Not so fast, tough guy," I said, wrapping my palm around his wrist and squeezing tightly.

"Oh, look who it is! The pretty boy himself." Bruno gave me a twisted smile only a sick fuck can make.

"Shut the fuck up, Bruno."

I used my free hand to pull Lynx close, examining every inch of her. "You okay?"

She nodded, her gaze on the ground.

"Look at me." When she didn't, I gave her a little shake. "Look at me."

Of course, Bruno probably thought my attention was completely diverted, and he tried to skip off. No such luck. I'd been a fucking bouncer for too many years to fall for that one.

"Not so fast, Bruno." I grabbed him again and dug my fingers into a pressure point in his wrist. His knees buckled a bit but I wanted him alert, so I let go a touch.

"Lynx, look at me!" This time I demanded her attention and got it. "Tell me what this ass wanted."

Not meeting my eyes, she muttered, "We're making a scene."

"I don't give a shit. Tell me."

"He wanted to know what I've been up to."

"And?" I asked her, ignoring Bruno's wince as I squeezed his arm tighter. "He mention the sheik?"

Silence.

"Huh?"

"Yes," Lynx hissed.

tinged

"Hmm, I thought I made it clear a while back, namely when I told you to get the hell out of town, to never utter his name again?" I eyed Bruno, and he refused to meet my gaze.

"It's my business, dude," he squeaked out.

"Not anymore." I let Lynx go and said, "Go to the hotel. Call Sampson at the club and tell him to meet me at Landon's in Lauderdale. He'll know where it is."

I dragged Bruno with me to the curb, letting out a sharp whistle to hail a passing cab.

No matter how hard he tried, Bruno couldn't wriggle out of my grip. Without his gun, he was no match for me. He was nothing but a washed-up has-been, a weak excuse for a man.

Over my shoulder, I told Lynx, "I'm taking a cab to Lauderdale, so tell Sampson to bring me a shirt and drive a car up."

The taxi wheeled over to the curb, and I dragged Bruno inside with me. "My buddy, Landon, he's with the Feds," I told him. "He's going to take extra-good care of you."

Based on the look on Bruno's face, it was almost as if I were the lesser of two evils when it came to him being on the wrong side of the sheik.

LATER THAT night, Landon slapped me on the back. "Thanks, bro. Not exactly what you thought would happen when you went out on a run, huh?"

"Not exactly." I took a deep breath and smoothed my hand down the front of the track jacket Sampson had brought from my office.

"We got enough from his confession to keep this guy for a while. If his shit turns out to be good, we'll have even more on him. Until then, we'll be keeping an eye on him if he gets out of here."

Not convinced, I eyed Landon, and he chuckled.

"Don't worry. Lynx will be safe. This dude will more than likely be going nowhere fast, but if so, we'll know it. Keeping eyes and ears on him."

"Lynx finally moved in with me, but I'm not with her all the time. I'm thinking about having one of the bouncers go around with her."

"She gonna stand for that?" He leaned back against his desk and scratched his scruff.

"No."

"That's what I thought. Sammy says she's tough, a hard shell to crack through."

"Pretty much, but I always liked a challenge."

Landon laughed at that and pushed off his desk to show me the exit.

Sampson was waiting for me outside, smoking a cigar. "Cuban," he said as he winked at me. "The Feds got all the best goodies."

"I'm sure they do. Let's roll." I opened the passenger door to the SUV. "I need a fucking shower and to see my woman. You talk to her?"

"Yeah, boss. She's good, at your place. Doesn't know you got Jovi stationed downstairs."

"Good."

Dusk was falling as he pulled onto the highway, the buildings lighting our way back south.

I glanced at him. "You need to hire one or two more guys. I'm going to need someone stationed there a lot."

Sampson nodded. "Figured as much."

That's how I knew Sampson was good people. He didn't question me, just let me be. He'd been that way since day one, something no one else had ever done for me until I met Asher.

"You know what, Sampson? I may have grown a pussy recently, but if I never told you before, welcome to the family, the Tunnel family. It's the best fucking family to be a part of—"

"I feel you, man," Sampson with a grin.

Leaning my head back into the headrest, I closed my eyes and prayed for my woman to be okay.

More than okay.

thirty-two

OPENING NIGHT arrived. It was a soft opening during the late fall—
the not-so-busy season—traditionally the calm before the storm
surge of winter-break vacationers.

Asher had arrived earlier in the week, just him and Natalie without
the kids. He was content to hole up in a suite with his woman and not
micromanage me, which made me happy. I was confident everything
would run smoothly—the hotel business was in my blood.

I'd never felt more fucking confident than recently. My ego savored
the fact that I was my own man, doing shit on my terms. But mostly it
digested every morsel the woman currently getting dressed placed in
my hand.

Lynx had spent at least an hour in the bathroom doing God only
knew what with her hair. I sat on the balcony, my tux shirt undone
around the neck, my bow tie not even close to being tied, dreaming of
not showing up to the event, burying my face between her legs, licking
and sucking her every drop of wetness.

"Hey."

When I heard her voice, I turned, completely unprepared for the
sensational beauty I would find. Wearing a green dress, the color of

grass on a well-manicured golf course, vibrant against her slightly tanned skin, soft and flowing around her luscious curves, Lynx looked like royalty. Her hair was smooth and pulled into some type of updo arrangement, and on her feet, sky-high gold metallic heels that I wanted to toss into the air while I buried myself deep inside her.

My mind was working overtime imagining the scenarios.

It couldn't be helped. I had to adjust myself.

"Lynx." Her name caught in my throat. "You look beautiful. No, stunning. Ravishing. Come here," I demanded, my voice hungry with need, my thoughts jumbled like a blanket on a windy beach. When she hesitated, I said, "The breeze is gentle, your hair will stay in place."

She smiled and stepped onto the balcony. My arm swooped out and pulled her close as soon as I could reach. "Mmm." I breathed her scent in.

"I like your shoes," she told me, smiling toward my black-on-black-patent Air Force 1s.

I shrugged. "You know what they say. You can dress up a bad boy, but you can't make him wear loafers."

"I'm not sure that's how it goes," she said, giggling in my ear. Her giggle—it had been a long time, but it was slowly making a return. I'd pay a cool million for each and every one if I could.

"It's absolutely how it goes, or maybe I lost all my brain cells when you walked out in that dress, looking the way you do. All sexy and needing to be fucked."

Another giggle and then a scowl. "Mike, that's not exactly the look I'm going for."

"It works for me." I ran my nose along her cheekbone. Giving her an Eskimo kiss, I asked, "Ready to go?"

"Not really. I'm a little nervous, you know."

"It's going to be great. No worries. Nat's gonna be there. You'll really get to know Petey, Asher's brother. Looks a bit like him. Do you remember him from Vegas at all?"

"And your mom and dad'll be there."

"Ignore them. They'll more than likely both be bellied up to a bar and three sheets to the wind."

I laced my fingers with hers and squeezed, ignoring the pearls around her neck. They were meant to be some sort of peace offering from my dad. I let them go when I heard her next question.

"Do they know what I did? Before?"

"They don't, but it doesn't matter. I know and I don't care. You're who you are, and I love every bit of that person."

"When the book—"

"When the book comes out, no one is going to be prouder than me. Proud as fuck," I said firmly.

Lynx had been making progress with her therapy. As for me, I had to go with her a few times, mostly to make me understand that it wasn't my job to keep telling her to leave everything in the past. Lynx's experiences had shaped her, and it was my job to accept and understand that. We'd both been emotionally abandoned as kids. I'd clung to Asher and the Electric Tunnel gang, and Lynx went looking in all the wrong places.

While it was in the rearview, I had to acknowledge it existed.

I was reading parts of Lynx's story as she wrote it, and I couldn't lie—it was hard at times to read it, but she was mine now.

We were each other's for life.

"You know what? On second thought, I'm not so anxious to blow this joint." I ran my lips over hers, allowing my hard to melt into her soft.

A soft moan came from Lynx, granting my tongue entrance to her mouth.

"God, I never stop wanting you. It's never enough," I mumbled, our lips and tongues in a full mash-up. Sliding her dress off her shoulder, I traced her clavicle with my mouth. While bent at the knees, I explored her soft skin, ending with sucking on her breast. Careful with her dress, I pushed it lower, latching onto her nipple, sucking and nipping, laving and revering, before covering her up once again.

Not giving a good goddamn, I hit the floor in my tuxedo pants, barely feeling my knees on the balcony as I hoisted her dress, shoved her panties to the side, and worshipped Lynx with my tongue.

I looked up and caught a glimpse of the gorgeous woman in front of me, her head tilted back, her hair still perfect as I devoured her. I took my time with her most sensitive spots, not feeling hurried at all.

"Michael, Michael," filled the air around us.

I didn't slow or stop until my name was replaced with short pants against the darkening sky.

After putting her panties back in place and smoothing her dress, I stood and brushed off my knees, taking my time licking my own lips clean.

"That was—"

"Perfect," I said. "Fucking perfect. So fucking perfect. Now, let's go check on my hotel."

She ran her hand over her hair. "What about you?"

"Oh, babe, that was for me. All me. Don't you worry."

"If you say so."

"I know so." Winking, I grabbed her hand, the smell of her satisfaction a fervent perfume clinging to her skin.

This way, there would be no confusion who'd made her happy tonight.

"One sec," Lynx said, stopping me. "I have to fix my lipstick." She held a small tube of fuck-me red to her lips in the hall mirror and carefully applied the color for the second time of the evening—and we hadn't even gone anywhere yet.

I led Lynx to the elevator. She trailed behind me, holding my hand in one of hers, her purse in the other. Secretly, I was glad she was behind me. I was sure if I looked at her ass in that dress for one second more, we'd miss the party altogether.

"I'm proud of you, Michael," Lynx said while tucked against my side in the elevator.

Tugging her closer, I just nodded.

"I am. This is a big deal."

"I wanted to do it for you, for when you came back."

Her red lips grazed my chin, and I hoped they left a stain of color. This way, everyone would know I was hers.

Still hand in hand, we walked to the car.

"All I thought about was giving you a good life when you disappeared. Asher and I came up with this, and it felt right. I want to make you even prouder."

M Y PEOPLE and I had been working on the party for weeks. As Lynx and I pulled up in front of the hotel, a big spotlight roamed the sky, and white twinkly lights decorated the entrance.

Bobby, the valet greeted us. "Mr. Wind. Ms. Lynx."

"It's Big Mike and Lynx to you, Bobby. We're not that way here. Save the professionalism for the guests." I tossed him the keys and escorted Lynx inside.

The hallway was draped in white and silver fabric, candles marking our way to the back of the first floor. With the glass doors wide open, you could see clear out to the ocean. Hammocks hung over the grass and sand, with a large patio filled with tables and several bars in the center.

"Stunning," Lynx said softly. "The party staff outdid themselves."

I nodded with satisfaction. "They did."

"We did it, man."

I felt a palm slap on my back. Turning, I found Asher. True to style, he was wearing jeans, an untucked tuxedo shirt unbuttoned at the collar, and motorcycle boots.

"Looking dapper," I teased.

"I'm always going to be a ghetto rat." He winked. "A rich one, though."

"You're a good man, Asher Peterson. You've got nothing to prove to me," I said, staring him down.

Asher ignored my comment, leaning in to kiss Lynx on the cheek. "Gorgeous as always. Your sister coming?"

"Yes, she wasn't going to turn down a weekend here with Landon."

"Good to hear. Look at this place," Asher said with pride. "My Quinn is going to have it all one day. Mike'll be his mentor."

This got a chuckle from me. "You're not quitting anytime soon, old guy."

"He says the same bullshit to me about LA, the old fogey," Petey said as he joined us.

I chuckled. "Did you tell him to shut up?"

"Hell yeah." Petey slapped my back. We'd been bouncers together before we all learned he was Asher's half brother. Now he was a full-fledged brother and business partner. "But if he retires, more money for us, Mikey!"

"That's the spirit." I winked at Petey, and Lynx squeezed my hand.

"No fucking way, you two asses."

Natalie walked over to our group. "Hey there."

"Hey, doll. You having a good time?" Asher pulled her tight to his side, and I mimicked his move with Lynx.

"I am," Natalie said, "but you need to let Lynx and Mike get drinks. You're taking all their time. You too, Petey. Go mingle."

"I got you." Asher winked. "Go, kiddos, have fun."

"Shall we?" I tilted my head toward the closest bar, and Lynx nodded. "Wine?"

"Please."

"One white wine, a chardonnay, and a Jack on the rocks, please, Millie," I asked the bartender.

"Coming right up."

"Place is filling up," Lynx said. The patio was filled with Florida's socialites and a Who's Who of the hotel business.

"It is. Pretty damn amazing." I pressed my lips to her cheek, not wanting to let go of her.

"Hello, Michael," purred a familiar voice in my ear.

I turned and pasted on a smile. "Mother, nice to see you," I said as the prep-school boy inside me crept out.

"Beautiful job you did here. The decor is stunning."

"Thank you. Although Lila helped, we had a decorating staff, so don't think it was all me."

"I didn't," she said.

"Mother, meet Lynx."

"Nice to meet you, Mrs. Wind."

"Oh, I go by Darling. I shed that old bag's name as soon as I could." She eyed Lynx up and down, her gaze landing on the strand of pearls around her neck. "I see my son is treating you right. If I'm not mistaken, those are pearls exclusive to Wind Resorts."

I shook my head. "Actually, Dad sent them ahead of time as a congrats, or maybe just to be nice. Who knows with him?"

"That's your father," my mother said with a sniff. "Hot and cold at the drop of a dime."

As usual, my mother was stifling me with her backhanded nature.

Heat rose in my gut. Needing to cool off, I rolled up my sleeves, having abandoned my jacket in the car.

My mother ran her finger along my tattoo. "I see you're still into those crass tattoos."

"I quite like it," Lynx said sweetly as she ran her hand down my other arm.

I can't begin to tell you what that did to my ego, having my lady take up for me against my mother.

"See, Lynx loves it, Mom. Why don't you go and have fun. Eat some food, mingle."

"I think I will, love, but first, can you get me a gin and tonic?"

I called over to the bar, "Millie, do me a favor! Please take care of this special guest." I felt bad handing my mother off, but there was no way I leaving her with Lynx.

"Come on," I whispered to Lynx. "Let's go by the water and hide."

"No arguments from me," she said, leaning her head on my shoulder.

We stood on the edge of the property, listening to the waves crashing, our hearts beating in unison.

"You like Florida?" I asked. "See yourself staying here?"

"I like it. You're here, so yeah. Where else would I go?"

"Good, that's what I want to hear. I like it here, don't see myself going back to Vegas. That's my dad's town. Kind of want to make this mine . . . ours. If you'll have me."

She laid her hand over my tattoo—her smooth hand. She'd not cut into her palm in a few weeks, resisting the urge with daily meditation and eating apples. I'd learned the cutting was an addiction, like smoking or exercising too much. She could have eaten chips or fries, but apples were a healthier alternative.

"I don't say it enough. I love you," she whispered.

I didn't answer back with words, only with my lips against her much softer ones. We stayed like that for a while, my business coming together behind us, my future rolling out in front of us.

"Michael!"

And just like that, we were interrupted by the larger-than-life persona of my father.

"You must be Lynx. What a sight. Too bad I'm not twenty years younger."

When my dad flashed his veneers, I shot him the evil eye. He might have fucked Rochelle, but Lynx was mine now and forever.

"Pleased to meet you," Lynx said, not moving to even shake his hand. She knew to keep her touch all for me.

After his cheap come-on and brief introductions, our conversation actually went better than with my mom.

It ended with him saying, "Proud of you, son. Wasn't sure there for a while, but you really did something here."

thirty-three

LYNX WAS fired up as she left the party. There was something electric about seeing all of Mike's hard work come together—it did something to her insides. She was all turned out.

"Good night, you lovebirds," Lisa had called to them as they passed the reception area. She looked stunning, her blond hair blown straight, wearing simple makeup and a purple dress clinging to her curves. A far cry from when she worked with Lynx—something else she owed to Mike.

"Night," Mike said back when Lynx stopped to go hug her friend.

It hurt too much to consider how much she'd put Michael or Lisa through, so Lynx tried to make the new memories even more special. "Thank you," she whispered to Lisa across the marble desk.

"For what, honey?" Lisa's smile was bright, electric, blinding.

"For everything. Helping Michael, working here, being a good soul. I guess, thanks for being you."

"Aw, honey, go celebrate your man's success," Lisa said with a wink and a small shove to get lost.

Indeed, Michael's success brought a whole new breed of butterflies to Lynx's stomach as he drove the two of them back to *their* place. The condo had become somewhat of a refuge for their feelings and them, so they'd happily opted to not stay at the hotel for the night, giving up their weekend to Sammy and Landon.

It was hard for Lynx to wrap her head around, but she could now actually imagine living in a house with Michael. One day. For now, the condo was their place.

They rode up in the elevator, wrapped in each other's arms, sharing slow kisses. Inside their apartment, it became less gentle. Mike pushed Lynx into the wall, pulling her leg around his waist, leaving her to balance on one stiletto while he pushed his hardness into her soft curves.

With the hand that wasn't tight on her back, he shoved up her dress and pushed aside her thong—a replay of earlier in the evening. Except this time, his finger slid inside her. Then two. There was no gentle exploration or discovery. He found her spot and went for the kill. Within seconds, Lynx was moaning into his mouth, but he didn't let her off that easy.

When he drew his fingers out, Mike made sure Lynx was watching as he brought them to his mouth, the fine stubble on his face glistening. He licked both fingers clean, leaving not one drop to chance, all the while his gaze homing in on hers. His eyes were heavy with want, his chest rising and falling at an alarming rate—he was a man in heat.

Letting Lynx's leg fall, Mike dropped to his knees and slid her panties down, taking each leg out tenderly. Then his mouth was on her—again, another replay, but not tender in the least. He ravaged Lynx, his finger back in place, his tongue alternating between flicking and soothing her most sensitive spot.

This time, Lynx's head fell back against the wall as she moaned. "Oh God, Michael."

"Take it, babe, take all the pleasure," he mumbled against her, making her moan even more.

Only when he squeezed another climax from her did he roam back up her body, taking her dress with him, his tongue tracing its path. When his mouth returned to hers, Lynx tasted herself—a pleasure she'd only engaged in with him. With her sordid past, she took solace in this small fact. Treasured it like an expensive jewel.

She inhaled, breathing in Mike. He was all man and brute muscle, focused on her, content with pleasing only her. The idea was heady. Despite him having pleasured her twice, this knowledge made her hands shaky with need.

Lynx undid his pants and shoved them down. Mike kicked off his shoes and shrugged off the trousers, leaving him commando. She couldn't stop her hand from exploring his hard length, wrapping around the girth and applying just the right amount of pressure.

"Leave those shoes on," he grunted. "They're so fucking hot."

She wanted to ask if he was ready to take her bare. He hadn't yet, but they'd visited the doctor, and she received a clean bill of health and a birth control injection.

For some reason, she couldn't bring herself to ask.

"I want you," he said. "No barriers. You and me. Are you ready?"

And there it was—Mike's secret ability to read her mind.

She swallowed, nodded, and ran her hand down his cheek.

He didn't waste any more time with talking. Instead, he drove himself inside her, bringing her leg back around him. He took a few easy trips in and out, picking up speed, diving deeper. They were one, taking each other toward a place Lynx was quite certain they'd only been with each other.

Another jewel.

Totally spent, the pair crumpled to the floor, lying still in each other's arms.

"Want to take a bath?" Mike asked, running his hand down Lynx's bare back, stroking his fingers over her tattoo.

She knew he didn't need to see it to know where it was—he'd spent many Sunday afternoons memorizing its every intricacy. The quiet afternoon she'd pointed out the words CASH OUT, he'd made love to her on the spot.

Lynx gave him a small smile. "Yes, I'm all sticky."

He picked her up and carried her to the master bath. There he filled the tub, tossing in sample bath salts they had from the Firefly, and removed her shoes. When the water was to his liking, they settled in the tub.

Lynx leaned back against Mike's chest, breathing out a sigh of contentment.

"Perfect," he muttered, pulling her hair to the side. Whispering into her ear, he asked, "Marry me?"

The water was steaming hot, but Lynx couldn't help the shiver that ran through her.

thirty-four

Three days later

"MIKE, THERE'S a Benito Benzo here to see you."

"I'll be right out," I told the front desk attendant and hung up my private line. I strode out of my office wearing a T-shirt, Puma track jacket, jeans, and black patent Jordans. I was that kind of boss—a dressed-down one.

"Mr. Benzo," I said, greeting the small man wearing an Armani suit in my lobby.

"Mr. Wind." He offered his hand and I took it.

"Mike, please." Mr. Wind was my dad, and while he'd been both supportive and civil lately, I was my own man.

"Then Benito, I insist."

"Let's go back to my office. You brought something for me?" I cocked an eyebrow at his case and he nodded. Apparently, he was the best at what he did.

I led him back to my office and tossed my jacket over my chair, leaving my tattoo on full display as I pointed to the table. "Let's set up over here."

Benito set his case down and opened it. When the bright sunlight hit its contents, it set the room ablaze.

"Nice," I said.

"All of these are top quality and clarity, like you asked, and all are platinum set. I also brought a sizable selection mixed with different-colored stones as you requested."

Lynx had said yes, but it didn't mean that I wasn't going to get her a ring. I could afford the best, and that was what she was going to receive.

In my mind, the ring had to have some color—something warm and bright like her true heart. I gravitated toward a large emerald-cut diamond flanked by two yellow diamonds, bold like the sun, emanating warmth like the big ball in the sky.

A while back, Lynx had mentioned she was tinged, colored with something bad or some such shit. I hated hearing it. No fucking way was I letting her live the rest of her life feeling that way.

"This one," I said, tapping a finger on it.

"Good choice."

Benito packed up his case while I wrote him a check with a lot of zeroes.

"Nice doing business with you," he said as I walked him to the front entrance. "Send anyone my way."

CAME HOME to a dark condo. "Lynx?" I called out, looking at my phone.

It was after seven. After meeting with Benito and then showing the ring to Lisa, I had to head up a marketing meeting. I'd capped off the day dealing with a shitstorm over by the hot tub—a very angry wife had caught her husband vacationing with her best friend.

In all the excitement of the afternoon, I hadn't texted with Lynx.

She had plans to meet her therapist and then head to lunch with Sammy today. Lynx was supposed to be picking up some of her sister's pieces to sell in the hotel's boutique, and show Sammy the latest pages of her book.

Overwhelmed with the book and busy helping me, she'd put her degree on hold again, pushing her classes to the side. "I've learned more in the last few years than most do in a lifetime," she told me.

Considering the options where she could be, I tossed my track jacket and T-shirt in the hamper, changed into a pair of jeans with holes worn in the knees, and made my way to the bar. In my mind, if Lynx got home soon, maybe we'd stay in.

It wasn't until I was screwing the top off the Jack that a shiver swept over me. I didn't like that she wasn't home, hadn't called or texted.

Trying to tamp down my caveman instincts, I grabbed my phone and shot her off a text just as a call came in.

My stomach sank when I saw the call was from Landon.

"Talk to me," I demanded. "Where's Lynx? She was supposed to meet Sammy, and now she's not here."

"Listen, Mike, I'm in my car, heading to get you, and then we'll talk."

"No fucking way. Spill it." I paced the dark apartment, finally leaning my forehead against the window.

"We're going to fix this."

"What?" My question reverberated off the glass. "What the fuck are you going on about?"

"Bruno made a deal, gave the Feds some info about the other guys, the ones Zayid sends ahead of time. Apparently, the intel was good, and he was cut loose."

"Fuck it to hell, Landon."

"Of course, he was told to lay low, stay clean and honest, but you know he's an idiot."

"Where is my woman?" Thank God the window was made of safety glass, because my fist met with it three solid times in a row. Then a fourth for good measure.

"We're going to find her."

I growled, unable to form a sentence.

"They were at lunch, and Bruno walked right up to their table. Stepped behind Lynx, packing heat, and told Sam he'd shoot if she made a peep. Then he walked Lynx out of there."

"FUCK!"

"Sam is at home, in shock. I left an agent with her. I know you got your other girl in a safe house, but I'd warn her."

Lisa.

"What about my real fucking girl?"

"We're on it. Looking as we speak. I'm going to come get you, and we'll go from there."

"Did you call Carson?"

"On his way."

Of course, I was the last to know.

Trying to put a lid on my rage, I ground out, "I'm going to have Sampson go check on Lisa, but you better get here fast or I'm going rogue on this one."

I disconnected the call, called Sampson, and then punched the shit out of the mirrored shower door—which wasn't fucking safety glass.

thirty-five

LYNX FINALLY felt at peace. She'd dropped out of her classes but was helping Mike. He acted all tough like he didn't need any help, but it was an act. He wanted her help.

"I love your help, it's just I don't want to let you make any more sacrifices," he'd told her.

Bullshit. He loved it and she knew it.

The writing had been a pleasant surprise. She couldn't believe how much she loved curling up in a corner of a coffee shop and writing down her thoughts and experiences. She'd originally thought reliving them would be unsettling.

"This is really good. Your feelings jump off the pages." Sammy peered over the short manuscript as they were seated on the outdoor patio having a late lunch, iced teas in front of them and a bread basket in the middle of the table.

Together, they made some notes with a red pen, occasionally striking out parts that felt too intimate to Lynx.

"Do you think I should use a pen name?" Lynx sipped her tea and looked away, distracting herself from what her sister might think of her experiences, although she wasn't sure why. They'd compared notes,

tinged

and many of them had been the same.

"No. This is too important. You can't be shamed by your actions, Lynx. You were making ends meet, and were very enticed by an opportunity. You were sort of young and foolish, because you also set out to find me. And you did."

"Landon did," Lynx mumbled.

"He did, but with the help of you and your friends. He fought a lot of red tape from the agency. Carson's old contacts and money made it all happen faster." When Lynx kept her gaze on her iced tea, Samara reached for her hand. "Look at me, sweetie."

Sighing, Lynx looked up.

"We're lucky to have found each other, and I'm so glad we did. We'll have that forever." Sammy spoke softly, her words blanketing Lynx with the warmth of unconditional love. "I'm proud of you, and so is Mike. You need to wear your story with pride."

Closing her eyes, Lynx imagined it—others benefitting from her story.

"Hello, ladies."

Lynx's heart stopped at the unmistakable voice that came from behind her. Something hard jutted into her back and she froze, afraid to move. Becoming all too aware of the deserted patio, which was creepily quiet, she felt her heart stammer in her chest.

"Nice to make your acquaintance, Samara," Bruno said. "I've heard all about you . . . at least when Lincoln here was loyal to me."

Sammy glared up at him, but kept her voice low. "I think you should go away."

"Not so lucky. I'm going to keep my piece right where it is—on your sister's back—and she's gonna leave with me. No fuss, no nothing. Hear me? Nod and smile if you do. Don't call attention to us, or I'll pull the trigger."

"Do it," Lynx said quietly, fixing a pleading gaze on Sammy. Her sister had just told her how lucky they were to have each other. Lynx would deal with this quietly on her own, and then have a future with Sammy. And Mike.

Oh my God. Mike is going to go ape-shit.

"Let's go," Bruno demanded. "I have plans."

He helped Lynx stand and guided her to the exit at the rear of the patio.

Lynx refused to turn and look at her sister. She kept putting one foot in front of the other, heading to the unknown, unafraid. She'd

159

survived a lifetime of crap . . . she'd outsmart Bruno too.

"What's your plan, Bruno?"

"Oh, you'll see, my dark-meat pretty." His voice was sinister, more outraged than ever before. A chill ran the length of her body at his use of Zayid's pet name for her, but she remained stoic on the outside.

"Here we are." Bruno unlocked a dark Cadillac and shoved her in the passenger side, never moving his gun from her. Keeping it trained on her, he rounded the hood and got in, locked the doors, and started the engine.

"Give me your phone," he demanded, his gun pointing at her face.

Cool air blasted from the vents as she reached into the pocket of her jeans shorts and pulled out her phone, just then realizing she'd left her tote with all her belongings at the table.

Bruno took the phone and tossed it out the window, then swung a U-turn and drove back, directly over it. "Let's hit the road."

He was quiet as he navigated the side streets. When he hit I-75 toward Tampa, he finally spoke.

"My friend only had to hang around Sammy's shop for a few days before he overheard her making lunch plans with you today. It was like winning the lottery. First thing I did was give Zayid's men a ring. You're worth a lot of money. I guess your sister was kinkier, but for some reason, he thought you were a real prize."

Resisting the urge to poke her palms with her fingernails and make herself bleed, Lynx stared straight ahead and considered her options. She could claim to need to use a bathroom and run, or she could throw herself out of the moving car.

Or she could wait for Mike. She knew her sister would call Landon. They would find her, and maybe, just maybe, wherever Bruno was taking her would lead to the larger pipeline for girls being sent abroad.

If she played along for a while, she could make Mike and Landon proud, lead them to the source. Rather than just dreaming about being the hero like she used to, she could actually be a savior for other women. And to do that, she figured she should act the part of a disgruntled kidnap victim.

"You sure you want to do this?" she asked.

Idiot that he was, Bruno told her his plan. "Oh yeah. I'm going to get my moolah and fly the coop. Caribbean, here I come. Sand, beaches, and women."

She shrugged.

"For your sake, I hope it works out."

tinged

"If I wasn't afraid of those assholes, I'd backhand you for that comment. But they want you unharmed." He let out a long cackle. "They think you're rushing back to get to them."

"Maybe I am." Lynx let her old professional voice come out—coy, sexy, and wanton. She hated the way it sounded, but it seemed to please Bruno.

They drove across Alligator Alley, and hours later made their way over the bridge and into Tampa. Bruno pulled up in front of a luxury hotel.

"Be good. I don't want to hurt you." He jumped out of the car and opened her door, taking a firm grip on her wrist as she got out. "Feel good? You should've felt the way your boy toy squeezed my arm."

Mike should have stayed out of it that day. Lynx kept her thoughts to herself and walked into the hotel.

In the lobby, Bruno urged her into an elevator and pushed the button for the seventh floor. Surprised he already had a room key, Lynx watched him pull it out and open a room.

He pulled some rope from his pocket and tied her to a chair, leering at her as he said, "Now we wait."

For a second, Lynx couldn't help but wonder what the hell she'd got herself into. She could be going back to that world, the one she'd escaped.

thirty-six

"**M**AN, I'M freaking the fuck out," I said as I threw open the door to my condo for Landon. "Where the hell is she? Do you have a lock on her?"

Landon crossed the threshold and ran his hand over his face. "Tampa. Let's go. We don't have time for chitchat."

"No shit. Tampa, what the hell? You let them get that far?"

My fist met with the mirror, shattering it—the same one Lynx had looked into to apply her lipstick a few nights ago. Pieces of glass went everywhere, raining down on our feet.

"Fuck! I knew I should've kept Jovi on her, but she caught him watching her and gave me hell."

"Mike, beating yourself up isn't helping. Let's go. I shouldn't even be taking you, but Carson assured me over the phone I was signing my death warrant if I didn't."

"At least he's right about one thing."

"For a preppy white boy, you've got a lot of street in you," Landon said as I slammed the door closed.

"Asher's more of a father to me than my own. And what the fuck? Preppy? Don't insult me."

He only nodded. There was nothing left to say. If Landon fucked this up, I was going to kill him, and he knew it.

"Don't be so cocky. This better work out in the end," I muttered when we exited the elevator.

Landon shot me a glare. "I didn't waste all that time over in the desert saving those girls just for them to go back."

He beeped open the doors on his black Escalade and didn't waste time gunning the engine. The flashing red law-enforcement light on the dash cleared traffic ahead of us, helping us maneuver out of the city fast, and before I knew it, we were flying over Alligator Alley.

Landon's phone went off every other minute or so, and he'd bark some instructions into his headset while nodding his head. "Uh-huh. Yeah. Feel me?" was about all I was privy to.

Unable to take it anymore, I slammed my fist into the dash. "What the hell is going on? Stop with all the calls and head-shaking and uh-huhs. Fucking tell me." I was good and sick of hearing only one side of every call.

"She's in a hotel in Tampa. We're already inside with a surveillance team, and Carson is working on getting a second one. Bruno's with her and armed. But he's alone and outgunned, so we're gonna get her out real soon."

"Tell them to do it already! What the hell are they waiting for? Go!" My voice boomed inside the car, and I didn't give two shits.

"We have to wait and see who's coming, catch him on something bigger, more incriminating. He doesn't have much more to give us."

"That's bullshit! Stop using Lynx as a decoy. Go in, or I'm going to when we get there."

Fishing my phone out of my pocket, I called Carson. "Man, what's with all this waiting shit? I want to get her out of there. Now!"

I heard all kinds of background noise on his phone and then it went quiet.

"I'm on my way," Carson said. "And you need to calm the hell down. I have a team watching. Let's see what Bruno is up to. If I didn't think it was safe, I'd say pull her, but we got eyes on her."

Gripping my phone so hard it might crack, I practically yelled into it. "No, I don't like it. Either you send someone to get her, or I am. I'm not joking, Carson."

I disconnected the call before he could piss me off any further.

"Go, drive faster," I yelled at Landon.

WE PULLED up across the highway from the luxury hotel where Bruno was holding Lynx, stopping in front of a small commercial building that looked empty. I eyed the hotel from the passenger side window. No one knew hotels better than me. I counted the floors, guessed where the emergency exits would be, and formulated a plan in my head.

Compared to the crap we used to pull as teens in my dad's hotels, this was cake.

"We got a surveillance crew inside here," Landon told me as we sat in the SUV, nodding toward the empty building next to us. "Got a camera on the room. Lynx is tied to a chair, but she's in no imminent danger."

I played dumb and continued to stare at the hotel. Chances were they were on this side of the building if his team could see them from here.

"Which room? Show me."

Nodding toward the building where his team was set up, he barked at me, "Let's go inside."

Who the hell did he think he was? My boss?

Opening my door quietly, I watched Landon open the trunk and reach inside. When his attention was diverted, I jumped out of the SUV and quickly ran across the highway to the hotel. Glancing back, I watched him slam the trunk and give me the finger. He couldn't holler for me—he'd call way too much attention to himself—so I was home free.

Bursting into the lobby of the hotel, I ran straight into my next obstacle. Literally. I was a pathetic sack of shit, not thinking straight, and absolutely no use to my woman.

"Sir? Mike? My name's Sam. I work with Carson. I'm going to have to ask you to calm down."

Why did Carson have to know me so well?

Shrugging his meaty hand off my shoulder, I walked like a good boy toward some conference room and showed myself in. Inside was a man talking on the phone.

"Yeah, he's here. We got him. Predictable, yep," he said, laughing into the phone.

Without needing to confirm he was talking about me, I gave him the finger. He laughed even harder before disconnecting his call and turning his attention to me.

"Just got word the sheik's right-hand guy went up to the room," he said. "Looks like you won't be waiting long to see your lady."

Wanting to break the hell out of here, I looked toward the door and the other agent, Sam, blocking the exit.

I pulled back my shoulders and puffed out my chest. Hell, if he wanted to see who had a bigger cock, I was game. "I want out of here. This sting is over."

As both agents shook their heads at me, the phone rang. The agent who'd been on the phone before answered it.

"Yup, Mitchell here." After being quiet for what felt like a lifetime, he said, "Got it," and hung up.

"Listen, sir." Hating to have to grovel, I cleared my throat. "That's my woman in there. I'm crawling out of my skin not being able to do anything."

"Calm your balls," Mitchell said. "Your guy Landon is already in place, waiting by the elevators. As soon as that trio leaves the room, they're done. All the exits have been blocked, so there's no escape for them. Pretty much, the idiot pimp did them in when he picked a room so high up."

Sam nodded and added his two cents. "Sit, pace, whatever the fuck you gotta do, because you're not getting out of here."

"Forget my balls," I said, my emotions churning out of control. "I'm going to grow a pussy soon with this bullshit. I'm a bouncer, you know? I manage some of the toughest clubs in the country." My fist met with the wall, sending cheap paint and drywall raining to the floor.

Mitchell shrugged and said, "Have at it," as Sam said, "We're keeping you here."

"Fuck you, Sam. Who are you? My fairy godmother?"

He didn't answer, further infuriating me, so rather than beat the shit out of him like I wanted to, I ended up pacing. My shoes ate up the burlap carpet, the friction I created picking up carpet fibers, making them stick to the synthetic soles of my basketball shoes. Needing to calm the fuck down, I stared at my shoes as I paced.

Deep in mindless thought, I almost didn't hear the phone buzz a while later.

"They got 'em," Mitchell said, and my head shot up.

"They what?"

"They have your woman, bringing her back here now as we speak. The pimp and the right-hand guy are gonna be off somewhere far, far away. Done and done. Happily ever after."

I tuned out the rest of what he said because the door opened, and in walked Lynx and Landon.

Suddenly, I couldn't move. My feet were glued to the floor as I watched her walk toward me in slow motion. Her head was on Landon's shoulder, his arm wrapped tight around her—and it should have been me.

Stunned, I couldn't stop staring at her, taking in her short denim shorts, wrinkled tank, and sandals, needing to reassure myself she was okay as she leaned on Landon. I'd never felt more helpless and useless in all my life.

"Michael." She stood in front of me, standing on her own.

Every emotion, thought, and feeling was lodged in my lungs, squeezing until my breath was nothing but a wheeze.

Swallowing, I pulled her close, all the way close, my hip to her belly. "Babe, fucking hell. Are you okay?"

She nodded into my chest as her tears seeped into my shirt. The agents floated off into the background; Landon was only a figment of my imagination. For several breaths, it was only the two of us—Lynx and Big Mike.

My lips pressed to the top of her head. "Lynx, baby, you okay? My heart barely beat all night."

She grabbed my shirt, fisting a handful and pulling me even closer, tighter, nearer. "Don't move," she begged, and I shook my head.

"I'm not. This is all my fault. I should've kept Jovi with you."

Her eyes finally met mine. "This isn't your fault. I can't even talk about that, so shut up."

"Lynx!" And just like that, our moment was broken, cock-blocked by Carson as he strode like a panther into the room, silent but deadly.

"You're a brave one." He tugged Lynx out of my arms and hugged her as he looked over at me. "Hold your fire, Mike. I'm giving her back."

He did, and she was back into my arms.

"You ready to roll out of here?" I didn't know where we would go or how we would get there, but I needed out of these four walls. I needed privacy and open air.

"Yes." Her voice was tired and hoarse. With her hair a mess, all wild and kinky, her eye makeup smudged and her bra strap slipping out of her tank—she'd never looked more beautifully disheveled and mine.

I pulled Lynx into my side and made my way to the door. "You're going to pay for keeping me in here," I told Sam.

"Looking forward to it," the bastard said with a smirk.

Landon said to Carson, "We're going to debrief in the local office."

tinged

"Do your thing," Carson replied as he followed us out the door. "I'm going to get these two home."

Best thing I'd heard all night.

thirty-seven

A N HOUR or so before dawn, Carson pulled in front of our building and put the SUV in park. The ride had been quiet. He knew I was mad at him for not letting me help, and being Carson, he completely ignored my sulking.

"Here you are, kiddies. Home, safe and sound. Don't do anything I wouldn't do," he said, chuckling.

Lynx stirred in my lap. I brushed the matted hair from her face, and she opened her eyes. She'd conked out as soon as we hit the Alley and hadn't moved since, probably the shock and adrenaline wearing off. Unfortunately for me, I was still pissed off and half-cocked to kill someone.

I tamped down my agitation and ran a hand over her cheek. "Babe, we're home."

She cleared her throat and sat up, staring outside the window, and nodded.

Carson, being increasingly more annoying, came around and opened the door like a limo driver.

"Madame," he said, holding his hand out for Lynx. When she climbed out, he pulled her into a giant hug. "It's all going to be okay, honey. It's over now. Lila is going to call you in the morning so you can chat. She went through something similar, and look at her now. It's all good in front of you."

Lynx practically fell into Carson at his words, her forehead braced on his shoulder, her hand digging into his arm. It was hard not to be seething with jealousy, but I reminded myself that Carson was family. At the end of the day, he was right—Lila had been through something similar, and now she was all good.

Carson finally let go of Lynx and sent her my way. "Mike, take care of your lady."

Thank fuck.

She came eagerly into my embrace, plowing her face into my chest. And that's how we walked into the building, Lynx leaning into me, her face on my shoulder.

Mine.

Upstairs inside our place, I gently braced her against the wall and placed a kiss on her cheek, her forehead, her other cheek, and everywhere else. All over her face and jaw and neck, I placed gentle and chaste kisses filled with promise.

"Michael, thank you," she whispered.

"I didn't do anything. It was all Landon and Carson."

"Babe." Her hand smoothed over my shoulder and down my forearm. "Without thinking of you, knowing you'd come, believing in us, I never would've made it through that. Never."

I can live with that.

"I love you," I told her.

"Love you back. So, so much," she said, breathing life into my soul.

Still holding her, I asked, "Are you hungry?" We'd had bottled water in the car, and Lynx had managed to eat a banana.

She shook her head. "I want to get out of these clothes."

"No problem. Don't look at this mess. I'll deal with it tomorrow."

Lifting her off the floor and cradling her in my arms, I carried her to the spare bathroom. Once I set her on her feet on the heated tile floor, she kicked off her shoes and I stripped her of her clothes.

"Garbage," she mumbled, and I tossed them toward the trash can. I'd take them out later.

Turning on the shower, I checked the water temperature and lifted Lynx in. Quickly getting rid of my own clothes and shoes, I joined her underneath the spray.

I took the lilac-scented soap Lynx loved and lathered every inch of her soft skin, water continuing to rain down on us. She tilted her head back and shampooed and rinsed her hair. I added some conditioner like I'd seen her do so many times, and combed it out, holding her close the entire time.

My entire life was inside the shower. The club, the hotel, the Tunnel gang . . . they were all important . . . but nothing like Lynx.

When she was done with her hair, I looked into her eyes, telling her without words what had just crossed my mind. She knew—I could tell she knew—but I said it anyway.

"There's nothing more important than you, Lynx. Nothing."

"Back at you, Big Mike," she murmured into my mouth, capturing my lips in hers, our tongues making love and our lower halves searching for friction.

"Michael," I mumbled back.

"Michael."

It was quiet but I heard it, and my heart picked up pace. So did her tongue, until I broke free for a moment.

"You okay with this?" Even though she'd started it, I needed to make sure. She'd been through a lot of shit today.

Widening her eyes at me, she whispered, "More."

I turned off the water and grabbed the towel off the rack, bundled Lynx, and carried her to the bed, my body dripping all the way. At least I remembered to toss back the covers before I spread her out on the bed.

Hovering over her, I ran my hand down her side, taking my time, allowing my fingers to tease her nipples and then adventure lower, running across her core before dipping inside her. She moaned, and I felt the sound all the way to my toes.

"Please," she begged, and I obliged, sinking deep inside my woman.

Rocking gently at first, we took our time, stretching out our satisfaction, taking pleasure in every movement. Until Lynx hooked her leg around my hip and dug her foot into my ass, and I couldn't control it anymore. I went faster, diving deep, the sound of our bodies slapping reverberating around the room until we both fell over the cliff.

Lynx went first, and I followed fast.

Afterward, we both lay there quietly, touching each other, holding each other tight until we fell asleep as the sun rose higher in the sky.

I T WAS mid-afternoon before I finally woke up and rolled over, finding Lynx's sleepy gaze on me.

tinged

"Hey," I said, my voice heavy with sleep and tension from the long, stress-filled night.

Lynx smiled and placed a kiss on my naked chest, her lips lingering. "What did I do to deserve you?"

Tipping her chin up with my finger, I said, "No way. It's all me deserving you. I must have made the gods happy." When she broke free of my stare and buried her face in my chest again, I asked, "You okay? Want to talk?"

She shook her head against me.

"No, you're not okay, or no, you don't want to talk?"

"I think I'm okay." Her lips tickled my chest as she spoke. "But I don't want to talk. I sort of feel like it's time to put this all behind me."

Pressing my lips to the top of her head, I decided to let it go. She'd talk and deal with this when she was ready. "Hungry?"

"Thirsty."

"Make yourself comfortable, and I'll be back. You want juice? It might be afternoon, but it's breakfast time for me."

"And coffee." A smile spread across her face as she settled back into the pillows.

"No prob."

I slipped out of bed and walked buck naked to the kitchen, made coffee, poured juice, and was back with a tray in hand. When I set the tray down, I caught sight of my jeans on the dresser and remembered what the hell I did the day before—before all the bullshit.

Snatching them up quickly, I shoved my hand in the pocket.

Score.

Lynx eyed me from across the room, watching every move I made.

"Have some coffee," I told her. "It's getting cold."

She shook her head, her eyes fixed on my hand, now holding a small black box.

"You want this?" I winked, teasing her. "Do you know what it is?"

She swallowed but said nothing, her eyes wide as she stared at the box in my hand.

Kneeling beside the bed, I said, "Lynx Whisper Bennett, will you marry me? I know I asked you the other night, but I wanted it to be official." When I cracked the box open, the stones caught the sunlight streaming in through the window, and sent sparkles dancing over every wall in the room.

Lynx remained silent, simply staring at the ring.

"Well?" I couldn't help myself.

171

Her eyes, brimming with unshed tears, met mine. "Yes! Yes, I'll marry you, Michael Anthony Wind."

Needless to say, the coffee got cold.

Later, I made a fresh pot while Lynx sat on the countertop in only a tank and underwear, her ring sparkling on her finger.

thirty-eight

"**M**IKE," BOOMED through my office phone when I answered, my feet up on my desk, the patio doors open, ocean air floating in. "What's up?"

"It's happening. Natalie's having the baby. Shit . . ."

"You've done this before, Ash. What's the problem?"

"I'm old. She's my world. I'm having a fucking fit. Get your ass out here."

I laughed into the phone. It wasn't often that Asher was rattled—I wanted to enjoy this for a minute or two.

"By the time I get a flight out of here, you'll have a new baby. You'll be okay."

"Don't be an ass. Get out here."

"What about Petey?"

I clicked on my computer and messaged Carson about the availability of his plane.

"Shut the fuck up. I love Petey; he's great. But, dude, I need you. Tonight, I'm going to be home with Quinn and the twins for the first time ever—alone." When I laughed, he said, "Yeah, yeah, cut your bullshit. I know I'm spoiled, but I need you. You're like a brother. More than Petey, but don't tell him," Asher said, rambling on for a long while.

By the time he finally took a breath, Carson had a flight lined up for me with a friend.

"I got you, Ash. I got you."

"And bring Lynx because I'm going to need her help with the kids. I don't know what the fuck I'm doing."

"I kind of figured that, you ass."

"Nat said I should call one of the girls from her gym or the club, but I'll look like an idiot."

"I feel you, man. I'm coming with Lynx. Gotta hang up so we can get moving."

He disconnected without another word, and I called Sampson. He wasn't affiliated with the hotel yet, but he knew how I liked shit done. I told him what was happening and asked him to come by while I was gone, check on my office and front desk, talk to the managers, see if there were any problems.

Then I texted Lynx, who texted back a bunch of girl emojis. I expected that one. She'd formed a sort of texting kinship with Quinn now that he was older and they'd reconnected.

By the time I got home to grab her and our luggage, Lynx was jumping in place, mumbling something like, "Baby time, and I'm going to meet Quinney's girl."

Lord help me.

As Lynx and I touched down in Vegas, our phones beeped simultaneously. Asher and Natalie were the proud parents of a brand-new baby girl, still unnamed.

A car was waiting to take us to the hospital, where we were greeted by Quinn, Lillie, and Parker eating candy in the waiting area—courtesy of Sadie from the Tunnel.

Sadie waved us over. "Hey, guys."

"Mike!" Quinn stood, holding out his hand and puffing out his chest.

"Come here, you idiot." I pulled him in for a hug. "I don't care if you're almost a man, you just became a big bro. Again."

"Hi, Quinney," Lynx said, causing the kid to blush.

"She called you Quinney!" Parker jumped up and down, hopped up on sugar.

"Pipe down, you little sh—, I mean squirt." Quinn tapped his little brother on the head.

"Hi, Lynx, 'member me?" Lillie stood tall and proud in a bright pink I'm the Big Sis T-shirt.

"I sure do." Lynx wrapped her in tight. "I'm here to take good care of you like I used to do for Quinney . . . I mean, Quinn."

"Yay! Mom had a baby. A girl, so everything is going to be pink! Dad's all grumpy and says he has three girls, including Mom, to make him crazy now."

"I bet he is." Lynx laughed. "Your dad is a tad overprotective."

Sadie caught my eye. "We were just up there, and then the nurse shooed us out so she could help Nat get more comfortable. I kind of got the gang all candied out."

"No problem. When can we go back up?"

Sadie started to answer me when her eyes caught on the door. I turned to see what captured her gaze, and of course, it was Billy. He was my replacement in Vegas, and another strip-club employee smitten with a dancer.

"Hey, Sadie," he said, shuffling some flowers in his hands.

"We had to leave the room." Sadie's gaze softened as she took in the flowers. "But those are beautiful."

Billy shrugged. "Yeah, I thought Natalie deserved something after pushing out Asher's fourth kid."

"Blech." Quinn pretended to throw up as Lillie and Parker ran in circles around Lynx.

"Okay, okay," I told Billy. "Why don't you two go home? We'll take the kids up soon and give Nat your flowers, and then take the kids home."

"I brought Asher's SUV with the car seats." Billy handed me the keys, looking mighty happy to get a baby-fevered Sadie to himself.

"Of course," I said like I knew what the hell I was talking about. "Car seats."

I really know nothing about babies or kids.

"Michael." Lynx put a hand on my arm, bringing me out of my head. "Let's go up. Worry about whatever you're worrying about later."

I nodded and tossed my arm around my woman, who had two kids holding onto one of her hands and Quinn walking protectively by her other side. Life was good, man.

rachel blaufeld
Lynx

L YNX PEEKED inside the hospital room and found Natalie lying in bed, a baby asleep on her chest and Asher out cold in the chair.

"Hey," Lynx whispered.

Natalie waved her in. The woman looked gorgeous, her brown hair brushed smooth, and wearing no makeup.

A commotion sounded out in the hall, and Natalie smiled. "Bring 'em back in. My brood."

Lynx went to the door and waved, and in walked the troops.

"Daddy," Parker yelled, wrestling Asher from his sleep.

"Hey, dude." Asher scooped him up and placed him on his lap, kissing his cheek. "You smell like peanut butter and chocolate. Where's my candy?"

"I ate it all!"

"You little sh—" Asher winked, and Natalie glared at him. "I mean, you should have."

Mike laughed. "Caught Quinn about to make the same mistake downstairs."

This time, Natalie turned her glare on Quinn.

"Who do we have here?" Mike leaned over the baby.

"This is Lulu." Natalie lifted the small bundle off her chest, and showed off the baby's perfect little face and sleepy eyes. "Isn't she perfect? Her eyes are light blue, so I'm hoping they go silver like her daddy's. That's what Parker's did."

Lynx walked toward the bed, her hormones in high gear. "Can I hold her?"

"Of course."

Lynx held the little baby until it was time to go, her only solace knowing she was able to play house for the next few days with the other kids.

She wanted a baby.

Bad.

epilogue

Six years later

LIKE SO many other mornings, Lynx walked barefoot onto the sand, waves lapping in front of her, the house quiet behind her. Raising her face to the sun, she welcomed its kiss on her skin, warming her from the outside in. She walked to the water's edge and stared at the horizon. A fine orange line dotted where the water met the sky.

This was her life. It was a good one, a beautiful one, and a special one.

A brightly colored one.

Her beginning had been rough, her middle an adventure, but from now until the end, it was meant to be radiant. She'd never imagined it would be this glorious.

An arm wrapped around her waist.

"Morning." Mike's voice was gravelly, the way she liked it. His front pressed firmly to her back, also the way she liked it.

Lynx felt safe and protected in the arms of her bouncer. Of course, now he was a legitimate businessman, but he'd always be her tough guy.

"Hey." She leaned her head back into his shoulder.

"You good?"

She nodded. "Just admiring the view."

"Me too." He squeezed her hip, and Lynx smiled. "You know what today is?"

His words tickled her ear. Another smile brightened her eyes, even though he couldn't see it.

"Our anniversary. A long fucking time ago, I went to a party in a penthouse atop a Vegas casino. I was a real knight in shining armor and stood up for a lady in distress. Turns out, she was my queen and I was her king. Just took us a while to figure it out."

Mike's breath was warm on her neck, and she let that and his words seep in like coffee in the wee hours. His hand grazed the small bump of her belly.

Lynx turned, the sun beating on her braids. "I love you, Michael Anthony Wind. Thank you for always standing up for me."

"Love you too, babe." He bent and kissed her, copping a feel of her ass all the while.

"Mom, look! Mom, look!"

Mike didn't let her pull her lips away for one more quick beat, and then she had to tear herself away to look up. Running down from the house came their son, Chandler, shirtless and wearing only pajama bottoms, all tanned with a head full of big brown curls.

"Mom!"

"Chandler," Samara yelled from behind him. "Let them be." She ran after him, but he was faster.

"Dad! Mom!" Chandler stood, catching his breath, a big smile on his face.

"Something's missing," Lynx said.

Mike looked up, tapping a finger on his chin. "Hmm, what could it be?"

"I lost a tooth," their son yelled, jumping up and down and kicking sand everywhere. "Aunt Sammy was there, drinking her coffee, texting with Landon, and pop . . . out it came!"

"Were you a tough guy?"

"Yeah, I'm Big Chandler because you're my dad, and you're Big Mike!"

"Morning," Samara said. "I tried to keep him up there and let you two have a moment. Sorry."

"Nah, it's all good. This is what it's all about." Mike ruffled the curls on top of Chandler's head. "Landon good?"

She nodded. "He'll be home soon."

Sammy was staying with them while Landon was out of the

country on special assignment. He still enjoyed chasing the bad guys, especially after what Lynx and Sammy had endured. His character had to be renamed in Lynx's book since he was still undercover, but she hoped one day she could write his story.

Truth be told, Lynx loved having her whole gang together. Why else would Mike buy a gargantuan house? He might like his alone time with his wife and son, but she'd never had a big family . . .

"Did you call Lisa?" Lynx bent down and kissed the top of her son's head.

Chandler shook his head. "I'm gonna call now."

"You know she'll be upset she wasn't the first to know."

Chandler nodded. "Because I'm named for her, I know, I know. But I don't get why we don't call her Chantilly."

"One day, tough guy." Mike picked up his son and kissed him on the cheek. "Come on, you can call from my car. We can go check on the Firefly together."

Chandler's eyes grew wide. "Can I get breakfast there? I want pancakes. Then I can swim! Please?"

"Yep, you can have whatever you want, my son. All you have to do is be respectful and proud of your mom."

Chandler grinned at Lynx. "She's a queen."

"Damn straight she is."

Lynx narrowed her eyes at her husband. "Michael."

"What?" Mike said with a big grin. "I only said damn. Let it go. He lost a tooth today; he's practically a man."

bonus epilogue

Landon

I SANK INTO the soft leather of Carson's private plane, pretty fucking happy with my decision. I'd spent a long time at the agency. Longer than I'd ever expected.

After getting those girls out of that godforsaken place, I couldn't let that shit go. I knew everyone had their dragons to slay, so I kept mine locked up tight . . . except when I talked with my shrink once a week. She'd heard way more than she deserved to hear, but when I realized I was falling for the beautiful Samara, I had to slay my own demons.

What I'd seen and heard—as well as what I was continuing to witness working for the agency—it all needed to come pouring out.

Unable to stop working for the government just yet, I continued traveling, fighting for what was right, gaining intel, helping to rescue beautiful young women who deserved way more than what they were given in life. But none of them captured my heart like Sam. She was the one for me, and lucky me, I was the one for her.

She'd made a name for herself in Las Olas, successful in her business there. Since I was traveling so much, she spent more and more time at Lynx's place when I was gone. She didn't know the details of my missions, but I was glad she was safe and happy while I was gone. There was no reason to trouble her with the knowledge of the countless other women still trapped overseas in the trade.

"We have Wi-Fi on board," the flight attendant said, interrupting my thoughts.

"Of course. Thanks," I muttered, then pulled out my phone and texted Sam.

Landon: Hi, baby! On my way. Looks like you and me are going to spend a lot more time together.

It didn't take long for her to text back one of those bitmojis with her caricature reading HAPPY RETIREMENT.

Yeah, I was going civilian. *Sort of.*

Carson had offered me a job about a year ago. He was expanding, bringing on a few other investigators, mostly young guys. He said he needed someone older and more experienced on the East Coast who could keep an eye on the young bucks, which was where he said I came in.

It took some convincing on Carson's part, but when Sam came home crying from the store one day last week, telling me she was pregnant—I knew.

I was done.

Sam had been in love with her nephew since he'd been in Lynx's belly, and now she would have her own child to cherish. Our child. And the last thing I wanted was to be an absentee father. So now I was the next PI in Carson's empire.

He called me *the old guy.*

"Can I get you something to drink?" the attendant said, interrupting my thoughts for the second time.

"I bet that suave ass has some top-of-the-line shit onboard." I smiled and she nodded. "Bring me something good. I'm celebrating a new lease on life."

"Coming right up. Congrats, by the way."

"Thanks."

What she didn't know was all the women I helped—they were my real reward.

Especially my wife, and now my unborn child.

Sneak Peak
smoldered

prologue

Natalie

I WAS THREE and he was eight the day his mom dropped him at our neighbor's house and never came back. Of course, I was too young at the time to remember that part of the story, but Mom talked about it. A lot.

"Cards were always stacked against that Peterson boy," she'd say. "Daddy gone, nowhere to be found, then his rotten momma up and left that sweet, innocent little boy. Hope he turns out all right, but sure looks like he's gonna have a lot of uphill fighting to do."

Once my childhood memories actually started to stick with me, there wasn't one without the "Peterson boy." Asher and I lived next door to each other from the moment his momma left him, and together we caused a lot of trouble. Well, to be truthful, I'd watched while he'd done most of it. My mother wasn't sure if our spending so much time together was for the best, but what other choice was there? Our little neighborhood was an extended family, all of us kids constantly being thrown together.

Although I'd forever be "the little stinker" in his mind, for me he'd always be "the one." He was the one I'd watched grow into a man while I was still considered a little girl, the guy of my dreams no matter how badly he behaved, the measuring stick against which every other man in my life would be judged.

As a teenager I'd watched him from a distance every chance I got, keeping an eye on what the other girls had done to get his attention. When I tried a few of the moves myself, the stubborn man had just laughed at me.

As a young woman, I settled with having him as just a friend, snug in my memories, until I couldn't do it anymore. To protect my own heart, I stayed away from him, completely dropped off his radar. For the last five years I had left him alone, hadn't kept in touch, even when I'd needed friends the most. Until, that is, when our paths crossed again on one awful, dreadful night.

I'd known Asher Peterson and had loved him from afar nearly my whole life, yet since we'd last seen each other, he'd grown into a man—a beautiful man—with a larger-than-life personality. And I wasn't ashamed to admit, he had me salivating the minute his face was once again in front of mine.

Then he spoke to me, and it was all over.

BREAK POINT

prologue

Jules

I T WAS a breezy day in late March. Gray clouds folded over the sky, blocking the sun. The temperature was mild for this time of year in Ohio, and sweat dripped down my back as I beat the living hell out of the wall in front of me.

With the ball, of course.

I'd lost track of how many forehands I'd done. Probably two hundred. My shoulder ached, and my palm was a sweaty mess from gripping the racquet. Tossing the grip into my left hand, I wiped my right hand clean on my shorts before grabbing a loose ball off the ground. Like a robot, I began punishing my other shoulder with one-handed backhands.

"Excuse me, are you going to be using the wall much longer?"

Looking up, I saw a guy. Yuppie, mid-twenties, slim but muscular, brown hair underneath his Ivy League hat, and a worn gray T-shirt.

"I'm actually finished," I replied, leaning over to snag a few stray balls and my racquet cover from the ground.

"I didn't mean to make you leave." His eyes bore down on me—chestnut brown, warm, and inviting.

Kindness radiated from him, which was something I hadn't experienced much of recently. I didn't know if I wanted to run from it or snatch it in my grasp and never let go.

"It's cool. I actually have something I need to do." I decided on the former. Running felt safer.

Plus, I do have something. Something I don't want—at least, I don't think I do. Who knows?

My mind was like that nursery rhyme . . . five little monkeys jumping on the bed, until one fell off and hit his head, or however it went. My ideas pinged and bounced about my brain until eventually they all fell flat like worn-out tennis balls.

"You're pretty good." The stranger cocked his head toward the wall, telling me he saw my earlier battle with the concrete slab.

I shrugged. My response wasn't exactly inviting, but he pushed on.

"I just moved here from Boston. Do you live nearby? We could play one day."

It was the first conversation I'd had with the opposite sex since the incident. I should have been more exhilarated or frightened, but instead I felt nothing. Standing here talking with this guy, I felt absolutely nothing.

"I'm working for the new tech company close to the university, app development. I haven't met too many people," he said, his matching Ivy League long-sleeved T-shirt stretching tightly over his chest. On paper, this guy must have been a catch.

Except my head was as cloudy as the sky. His forthrightness and honesty did nothing for me. Most young women would jump into this white knight's arms, but I'd learned to be cautious.

"Um, I'm not sure," was about all I could come up with in the moment.

"No pressure. I go in late on Tuesdays, so I usually come over here and hit. Maybe you'll be back next week."

"Maybe. I might be going back to school . . . college," I offered without further explanation.

"Either way, the invitation stands."

Mr. Ivy League opened his can of balls, slipped his Prince racquet out of its case, and began stretching. He twisted from side to side at the waist, working out the kinks in his lats, taking his racquet with him.

"See you," I called out when I caught a glimpse of bare skin above his shorts. Sadly, I didn't feel a tinge of desire, or anything really.

Walking back to my childhood home, I made a mental note to never hit at the park on Tuesdays. My high school coach had been begging me to come play, to hit a few balls or whatever. His offer was starting to appeal to me. Especially on Tuesdays.

As I walked back into my house, a voice called from inside, "Hurry up, Juliette. The new coach will be here soon, and this isn't something we can pass up."

"Okay, Mom. I hear you."

"I don't think you do," she said as she walked down the steps, a cup of tea in her hand and a smile fixed on her face. Genevieve Smith cared about two things: my dead father, and getting me educated and out.

She'd isolated me from my peers most of my life with constant tennis lessons and tutors to ensure I did well in school, all in the hope of getting a scholarship. Then I'd squandered my first one. It was time to forget all that monkey business and move on. That's what she'd said when she took away my phone and the small life I'd created before it all went to hell. This time around, she meant business.

"I hear you, Mom. Now I need to shower and hurry back down, so if you wouldn't mind . . ."

With my hair still tied in a messy knot on top of my head, I scrubbed myself clean—showers had become perfunctory—and threw on a burgundy off-the-shoulder sweatshirt and black leggings. I dragged some mascara across my lashes, brushed through my hair, and tossed it back into a messy bun.

I was walking down the stairs when I caught sight of a broad-shouldered figure coming up the walkway. There was a knock at the door as soon as I hit the bottom step.

"Get it, Juliette," my mom called from the kitchen.

Opening the door, I was met with the exact opposite of the guy I'd just met in the park. This one was wearing dark jeans and a polo, and had longish hair, tanned skin, and the bluest of blue eyes.

"Hi. You must be Juliette. I'm Coach King . . . Drew. I took over at Hafton last season. The tennis program," he explained, mistaking my immediate crushing and infatuation for confusion.

The words clogged my throat, embarrassment flushed through my veins, and I was sure my cheeks were the color of my hair. It was the basest of attractions, purely physical, something I'd definitely never experienced.

After all, I was only twenty. That was normal, right?

I wasn't meant to fall like this when I was so young. Who the heck knew? My mom had certainly never prepared me for these things, or helped me navigate them. Her cold, austere parenting style was only warmed by my father when he was alive.

"You were expecting me, right?" The coach cleared his throat and glanced at an oversized watch on his wrist.

Underneath his bad-boys looks was quite a gentleman, no doubt the polished product of a prep school. No match for my sheltered suburban-public-school-educated upbringing.

Kind of like California. As if that wasn't mistake enough—signing up for that West Coast lifestyle—I was falling into some kind of blissful spell over my coach-to-be. We hadn't even spoken more than a few words to each other, and my body was humming as a result of my indecent thoughts.

"Um, hi," I said awkwardly, and added a lame little wave.

My mom picked this moment to come striding out of the kitchen, making an entrance.

"Genevieve Smith." She held out her hand. "And you are?"

"Coach King."

We were all still crowded around the threshold, the chilly air making its way inside, which was fine because I was hotter than a fire in hell. And I should know. I'd been to hell, and I was pretty certain I didn't want to go back.

Until now.

"I thought the coach at Hafton was older?" Looking King up and down, my mom inquired about the older coach as if this was all about her. And like everything in my life, it was.

"You mean Ace, Coach Hall? He retired two years ago. I helped him out for a year, and then they gave me the gig full-time. Actually, I was the one who reached out to you. I saw some kick-ass tape of Juliette playing. Pardon my French."

My mom rolled her eyes at his forthrightness.

I was fascinated with King's white smile, his biceps, and his not-so-muted attitude. Although he could have been muttering, "Blah, blah, blah," for all I knew, and I would have been spellbound. Something naughty and oh-so-right was simmering in him, just beneath the surface, clamoring to get out.

"May I come in?" he finally asked.

"Yes, yes. Come into the kitchen," my mom suggested. She offered cold drinks and left the two of us sitting across from each other at our butcher-block table.

"Tell me about yourself," he said.

I want to swim in your eyes. I haven't had a pulse since I left California . . . until now . . . with you seated in front of me.

I felt all of those soul-infused words deep in my belly and slowly rising in my throat. Before they came bubbling out, I tamped them down.

Instead, I said, "Sophomore status when it comes to sports. Tennis player, twenty, failure."

"Hey."

The deepness of his voice set off a ripple of lust through me. When his hand settled over mine, I stared at his calloused fingers and insanely sexy forearms. I wanted to run my fingertips along the veins and stroke his calluses with my thumb.

"You're going to have a second chance, and I'm going to make it happen."

I nodded, my gaze glued to his hand on mine. When he swiftly pulled back, probably realizing the inappropriateness of his action, I felt barren, empty, dejected. Between the chilly assault in California and my mother's cold attitude, I was drawn to King's warmth and kindness like it was a fireplace on a snowy day.

I tried using Jedi mind tricks to make him put his hand back, but he didn't. He spent the next half hour asking me about how much I'd been playing, and discussing tennis strategy with me. Never once did he bring up the incident at my old school.

"You need to get registered for classes, and I'll text you when I think would be a good time for you to watch a practice."

"I don't text. No cell phone."

"Then I'll call you," he said, standing to leave.

Yes, please.

acknowledgments

These always get too lengthy, and does anyone even read them? Seriously, someone e-mail me and let me know!

In an effort to condense, I will quickly mention a few (hundred) people and give thanks.

Several of my team members have been with me since day one, which says a lot when you're publishing your ninth book! My heartfelt thanks to:

Pam Berehulke, my editor and trusted right hand in this business.

Sarah Hansen, my cover designer, who makes the package look gorgeous.

Emily and Stacy Tippetts, my formatters, who make sure this e-book works or this paperback is in the correct order.

Maryse Black, the first blogger to take a chance on me, and who has supported me tenderly since then and hosted a beautiful cover reveal for this book.

Queen Virginia Carey, Robin Bateman, Christy Pastore, Fabiola Francisco, and Terilyn Smitsky, who have all held my hand and let me cry on their shoulder at various times in this industry.

Nicole Snyder, my PA and better half. E-mail her first. Always.

And, of course, my family. Xoxoxo.

There are not enough thanks for these beautiful people (after all, they put up with me):

Lisa from TRSOR, a true friend and business sounding board.

Sara Eirew, for the stunning photo on this cover.

My betas, who still love me.

The FTN Crew. Enough said.

Jennifer Dicenzo and Michelle Tan, the fabulous-est gals around.

The After Dark Ladies—Michelle, Yaya, and Grace—who make me smile daily. That's not easy when dealing with a broody author.

All the bloggers who give tirelessly to this industry despite the constant eruption of chaos. I always try to name all of you and inevitably leave someone off. So, here's to all of you.

And to YOU, the reader! You're the most important person around. Thank you.

about the author

Rachel Blaufeld is a bestselling author of Romantic Suspense, New Adult, Coming-of-Age Romance, and Sports Romance. A recent poll of her readers described her as *insightful, generous, articulate,* and *spunky.* Originally a social worker, Rachel creates broken yet redeeming characters. She's been known to turn up the angst like cranking up the heat in the dead of winter.

A devout coffee drinker and doughnut eater, Rachel spends way too many hours in local coffee shops, downing the aforementioned goodies while she plots her ideas. Her tales may all come with a side of angst and naughtiness, but end as lusciously as her treats.

As a side note, Blaufeld, also a long-time blogger and an advocate of woman-run anything, is fearless about sharing her opinion. She captured the ears of stay-at-home and working moms on her blog, *BacknGrooveMom*, chronicling her adventures in parenting tweens and running a business, often at the same time. To her, work/life/family balance is an urban legend, but she does her best.

Rachel has also blogged for *The Huffington Post* and *Modern Mom.* Most recently, her insights can be found in *USA TODAY,* where she shares conversations at "In Bed with a Romance Author" and reading recommendations at "Happy Ever After."

Rachel lives around the corner from her childhood home in Pennsylvania with her family and two beagles. Her obsessions include running, coffee, basketball, icing-filled doughnuts, antiheroes, and mighty fine epilogues.

When she isn't writing, she can be found courtside, tweeting about hoops as her son plays, or walking around the house wearing earplugs while her other son, the drummer, bangs away.

To connect with Rachel, she's most active in her private reading group, *The Electric Readers*, where she shares insider information and intimate conversation with her readers:

www.rachelblaufeld.com
Twitter: twitter.com/rachelblaufeld
Facebook: www.facebook.com/rachelblaufeldtheauthor
Newsletter: www.rachelblaufeld.com/signup

If you liked this book, feel free to leave a review where you bought it or on Goodreads. Send me an e-mail when you do, and I will thank you personally!